Jake noticed the man in the dirty red velvet coat and beaver hat standing at the bar, a grimy burlap sack resting in front of him atop the oak. Ellis poured the man a whiskey and the man untied the string from around the neck of the gunny. Ellis peeked in and drew back his head sharply as if punched.

The man in the red velvet coat laughed.

Then Jake saw Ellis pointing toward the door, saying something to the man in no uncertain terms. The man in the velvet coat stiffened, then tied the top of his sack again and pounded his fist atop the bar before taking the sack and stalking out.

Jake stood away from the table and went to the bar. "What was that all about?" he said.

Ellis looked flushed. "Son of a bitch had a head in that sack. Told him to take it and get out of my place."

Suddenly, the man in the red velvet coat burst back in the front doors, this time with a pistol in his hand. He came straight toward the bar.

"This is for you, mister," the man said, and he fired . . .

R. H

Books by Bill Brooks

Dakota Lawman
THE BIG GUNDOWN
KILLING MR. SUNDAY
LAST STAND AT SWEET SORROW

Law for Hire
SAVING MASTERSON
DEFENDING CODY
PROTECTING HICKOK

DAKOTA LAWMAN
THE BIG GUNDOWN

BILL BROOKS

HarperTorch
An Imprint of HarperCollinsPublishers

❦

HARPERTORCH
An Imprint of HarperCollins*Publishers*
10 East 53rd Street
New York, New York 10022-5299

Copyright © 2005 by Bill Brooks
ISBN-13: 978-0-06-073722-1
ISBN-10: 0-06-073722-0

First HarperTorch paperback printing: October 2005

HarperCollins®, HarperTorch™, and ❦™ are trademarks of Harper-Collins Publishers Inc.

Printed in the United States of America

Visit HarperTorch on the World Wide Web at www.harpercollins.com

10 9 8 7 6 5 4 3 2 1

For Charles Price,
Writer, Friend

DAKOTA LAWMAN
THE BIG GUNDOWN

Prologue

❖

THEY DROWNED THE BOY AT NOON.

They trussed him up with rope and fence wire.

He struggled against them, but they were too many and too strong and they dragged him down off the back of the wagon and toward the creek.

He could smell the water before he could see it. Old water, ancient like time itself running through the cutbanks, a thick vein of brown blood it seemed like. They dragged him near to the edge that dropped off down to the creek where it was deepest, where the water had cut a deep hole that even in the summer when the water was less, it was still deep enough a man couldn't see down into.

"No! No!" he cried through swollen and broken lips. They had beat him severely.

One of them pulled his pistol, cocked and aimed it, brought the barrel close to the boy's dark sweaty face.

"You want me to shoot you, nigger? You want me to blow your brains out?"

"You gone kill me, do it quick," he cried.

The man brought the pistol barrel down hard across his face and it stung like a whip, like a razor slashing him.

His legs gave out and they pulled him up again. They forced him to look down into the water. He could see their shadowy figures in it, wavering like ghosts it seemed. The water looked cold, brooding and forbidding.

He could see where the water eddied around old tree stumps that had floated down from upstream some time or other. Just across on the opposite side a large branch lay snagged, the water working around it, catching, then moving on.

They cursed and slapped him across the face with their hats and when his legs gave out again, two of them took hold of him by the ankles and another by the neck and lifted him.

The man with the gun said, "Tie the end of that rope around his neck." The rope was wove out of horsehair and one end of it was knotted around an anvil they'd brought along, one of them carrying it from the wagon bed in his arms as he might a lost calf, straining under its weight.

They laid him upon the ground and kneeled on him so he couldn't rise up while one of them took the end of the rope, tied to the anvil, and wrapped it around his neck. The one with the pistol said, "Tie it up short, I don't want him floating like a snagged fish. I want him down under there."

They wore hoods made out of feed sacks with holes cut out for their eyes. He could see the whites of their eyes sometimes when the hoods shifted. He wondered why they'd hid their faces. He knew every one of them from their voices, and one by the boots he wore because of a pattern stitched into the shanks: a rose.

He'd worked alongside them, cutting hay, bailing it, herding cattle from one ground to another, branding them, castrating them, building line shacks, and putting a new roof on the bunkhouse where they all slept as hired hands. He'd played cards with them and drank some with them in town. He didn't understand why they were trying to hide their faces. It scared him more that they had.

The man tying the rope snugged it up tight around his neck without saying anything, but he was breathing hard.

"Why you doing this?" he said.

The man with the pistol leaned down so close he could smell the stink of whiskey and smoked tobacco on his breath. He tested the knot around the boy's neck, made sure it was a good one. Said, "Goddamn nigger. Don't tell me you don't know why. Don't insult my good intelligence or I'll gouge out your eyes with my thumbs before I toss you in that creek. You'll die without any eyes to see your maker."

Then the man balled his fist and smashed it against his nose, breaking it, and he could taste the warm salt of his blood leaking into the back of his throat. His left eye was swollen nearly closed from where they'd punched him almost senseless before tossing him in the back of the wagon. And one of them had struck him on the ear with something, a rock maybe, and it hurt worse than anything else, like something had bit it. He couldn't hear out of that side of his head.

"She was a decent gal till you got holt of her," the man with the pistol said, his face still down close. "Nobody'll want her now."

He started to speak, but the man smashed him in the mouth with his fist again, like he enjoyed doing it, like it gave him the greatest pleasure. A tooth fell into his mouth and he spit it out with some of the blood and it splattered on the man's stitched rose boots and he cursed him again for doing it.

"Lift him up, boys," the man ordered.

Three of them got him up in the air while the other lifted up the anvil and they shuffled him over to the very edge of the bank again where it dropped off about four or five feet to the water below.

"This is the right spot," the man with the pistol said. "That's a deep hole right there and that is where he'll settle, at least till next summer when the water goes low again."

He wriggled and twisted against their greedy hands and got himself free momentarily and hit the ground hard, but they picked him up again and the rope went tight around his neck as the one with the anvil pulled a little on it, choking him.

"Toss him down into that goddamn hole, boys."

The fear shot through him so hard and mean he began to cry, snot and slobber leaking out of him, mixed with the blood, as they swung him back once, then out over the edge of the bank and released him. He fell free momentarily before the anvil's weight caught and jerked him down.

The water came up around him in a cold rush. His whole flesh shrank from its cold.

He gasped for breath, but water rushed in as the anvil dragged him down. The water tasted foul, dirty, and he gagged on it, but when he did, more rushed in and he began to swallow, but he couldn't swallow fast enough.

Bolts of panic struck at his very heart, flooded his mind. *My god, no! No! No!*

But there was no escape from it. The more he fought the more water rushed into him. His mind blurred. He swallowed and swallowed that dirty putrid water and at last it felt as though something were releasing him. He twisted like a caught fish. He opened his eyes once and saw inches away the strand of rope that held him tethered. Then the darkness came into him and took away his struggle, his fear, his panic. All the rest.

The men on the bank watched as the bubbles rose to the surface, then were quickly swept away by the current. It reminded one of them of the bubbles a snapping turtle makes when it sets down on the bottom. They stood in silence, the wind whipping at their clothes, and one of them took off his hood and held it in his hand and the others did the same. The immediate violence had passed out of them and now their bodies had gone slack in the watching. They had turned into spectators of their own crime.

They waited four or five minutes, watching the place where they'd thrown the boy into the water, waiting to see if the anvil held.

"Maybe that current'll carry him downstream," one of them said.

"No, he ain't gone nowhere with that chunk of iron anchoring him down."

Then the oddest thing: The boy's boots floated up and they could see the lower half of his legs where the cuffs had pulled down, the bare brown calves.

"Shit," the man with the pistol said. "His whole bottom half is floated up. That anvil's got his top half weighed down, but not his legs."

They stood there wondering what they should do about this situation.

One of them tried poking at the legs with the barrel of a rifle he'd gone and gotten out from under the seat of the wagon, but it was too far a drop to effectively do anything.

"Somebody'll for sure come along and see him in there," one of them said—the one who'd carried the anvil. "They'll pretty much know who did it, seeing as how—"

"Shut the goddamn hell up," the man with the pistol said.

The boy's legs and boots bobbing on the surface would get pulled under, then resurface, the current tugging at them, then releasing them, again and again. The men were uncertain about what to do.

His name was Nat Pickett and his daddy had brought him west from Alabama to Oklahoma, where he first learned to cowboy and had a handsome way with horses. By the age of fourteen he was riding drag on a cattle drive that took him north into Kansas, where he got drunk for the first time and lost his virginity to a colored prostitute in a Hays bordello and once saw Wild Bill disarm two Union soldiers.

He drifted always north, refusing to return to Oklahoma until he could go back with more than what he'd left there with. He thought he might like to own his own cattle company someday, get married, have children, and ultimately become a well-respected citizen in a town of his choosing.

The white girl had not been part of the plan.

Now it was too late.

"Well, ain't nothing we can do about it now," the man with the pistol said. "Not one goddamn thing. What's done is done and if someone was to find him now, or later, it won't make a shit bit of difference, now, will it. And if they want to lay blame, then let them try. For we are all in this together. Ain't nobody gone to blame one of us for doing what we did once they know the story.

What that nigger boy did was a sin and a crime and all we did was do what the law would have. They'd hang him and he'd be just as dead as he is now. We just saved them all the trouble. And if that don't wash, then by god I guess we'll go to fighting with whoever it is wanting to pick a fight over what he did and what we did."

Nobody else said anything and they went and mounted their horses and the one who'd carried the anvil climbed up into the wagon seat and took the reins of the gray hitched to it.

The man with the pistol said, "I guess we'd be wise to keep this thing between ourselves. For one thing, I don't know how old Parker would take it if he found out about this. I think that wife of his has turned him into a weak sister, hauling him to church ever Sunday. He might see it as bringing trouble down on his head he don't want and cut us loose. So it's best we just keep this thing to ourselves."

He looked at them each in the eyes and saw they were in agreement. Jobs were hard to come by that time of year, with winter about on them. They all knew it.

"We best get on back," the man with the pistol said.

"What about these?" the man in the wagon said, holding up his feedsack hood.

"Shit, I don't guess we need them no more."

"You think he knew it was us," asked the man in the wagon, tossing away his hood.

"Who gives a damn did he know or not?"

"I think he knew it was us. I don't guess we even had to bother wearing them."

" 'Cause of her," the man said, tossing away his. "I dint want her to see our faces case she woke up, is why."

The man in the wagon nodded, then snapped the reins.

"I could use a drink," he said.

"Hell, I guess ever one of us could," said the man with the pistol.

They rode on toward town without hurry.

1

THE WAY THEY FOUND NAT PICKETT was they'd been hunting for geese.

Toussaint had invited Jake to go hunting with him.

"Karen wants me to hunt her a goose for Thanksgiving," he said. "And since she's inviting you to dinner, I figure you might want to help me shoot one."

"It's the first I heard about it, being invited to dinner," Jake said.

"Well, she told me to ask you. I figure two of us will stand a better chance of shooting a goose than if just one of us was to go."

"Goose, huh?"

"Said it's traditional in her family. She's German, you know how they are. She wants to give the boy a nice traditional dinner, I guess me and you too. She's over to Otis's store right now buying the rest of the works, candied yams and that sort of thing. Says all she needs now is a nice fat goose."

"I don't have a goose gun to shoot with," Jake said.

"Hell, I got a pair of shotguns."

"What time?"

"Need to be there when it gets light—the place where

the geese are. Meet me out to our place. We'll follow up along the creek to a little lake where I think we might catch a few of those suckers napping."

"About dinner . . ." Jake said.

"What about it?"

"You think Karen would mind if I brought a friend or three?"

The breed's eyebrows arched.

"Clara and her two girls," Jake said.

"Sure, bring 'em along. Little Stephen will be glad to have playmates."

"Okay then, tomorrow, your place, before daylight."

"A good hour or so before so we can make that little lake, be sitting there with our guns ready. They see us riding in, they'll fly off. We have to be there waiting for 'em."

"That's how you hunt them, huh?"

Toussaint shrugged, said, "Hell, I guess, I never did hunt any; it's just what I heard from some others who have hunted 'em."

"And if we don't get lucky?"

Toussaint looked toward the mercantile where his wife and stepson went.

"Hell, then I guess we'll feast on candied yams."

The next morning Jake rode through the black cold, the sky poked full of stars. That hour not even coyotes howled. Everything was asleep except for men wanting to go goose hunting.

He was still thinking about the supper he'd had the night before at Clara Fallon's house. Clara and her girls sitting around the table with him, talking amicably. He liked them all a lot, and being there with them like that caused him to feel halfway normal again. It didn't take very much imagination to think of them all as family.

Later, after Clara put the girls to bed, they sat and talked awhile longer. Then when he got up to put his coat on she stopped him, said, "Jake," and he knew what she wanted and she must have known what he wanted too.

"It's terribly cold tonight," she said. The wind had been bothering the windows all evening. They could hear it keening outside. It had a lonesome sound to it, like a train whistle or the howl of a lost wolf.

"You want me to stay, Clara?" he said.

She didn't say anything but instead took him by the hand and led him to the back bedroom and set the lit lamp there by the bed and he watched her start to unbutton her dress.

"I don't want you to think this is something I'd do with just anybody," she said. He liked how the light fell soft on her face, leaving some of it in shadows. He came and took her hands away and undid the buttons himself, slowly, allowing time for her to change her mind if she wanted.

"I don't think this is something you'd do with just anyone, Clara."

Her hands now free of the undressing stroked the sides of his face then brought it down closer to her own and their lips touched softly, as though they were old friends who'd not seen each other in a very long time. Their kiss was tentative at first, then they kissed again, their need more needy, and each time thereafter more still, even as his hands worked at the buttons, even as hers fell to raising his shirt over his head. As clothes dropped away, they found themselves in the most passionate of embraces. The lamplight flickered against the flocked wallpaper, causing their shadows to loom large until he reached over and turned down the wick and the light went out of the room and all that was left was just their breathing, their whispers to each other there in the darkness, their bodies entwined and falling to the bed. But he could still see her in his mind and she could see him.

She said his name again and he said hers.

And later he lay with her in his arms, staring into the darkness and wondering if he'd done the right thing. For trouble was still a hound with a fine nose that pursued him and wouldn't easily give up. And in spite of his not wanting to, he could not help but think of the last woman he'd been intimate with, the one who had betrayed him. And her betrayal would ultimately cause men to once again come looking for him, men who would either want to kill or capture him for a murder he did not commit, but one he could not prove himself innocent of either.

"Jake?" Clara said softly after long moments of silence.

He stroked her hair, said, "Can we just savor this moment?"

He could feel her nodding against his bare shoulder.

In a little while her breathing grew heavy and he was pleased that she felt safe enough with him to fall asleep, for to sleep with another was to be completely vulnerable.

He set a clock in his own head, a habit he'd learned when he had practiced medicine. It served him just as well now that he was the town's marshal. He'd set it for four o'clock and woke nearly precisely at that time and eased himself from the bed and dressed, sorry to have to leave the warmth and comfort of such a fine woman. But even if he hadn't promised Toussaint he'd go goose hunting with him, it was probably best that he not be found there in the morning by her girls. As the town's schoolteacher, Clara had a reputation she needed to protect. He did not want her to become the grist of rumor mills.

The steady clop of the horse's hooves on the cold hard-pan gave him small comfort in staving off the loneliness. The dark wind slithered through the grasses. Off to the west a sliver of crescent moon seemed almost biblical, as though he were some sort of wise man in search of the child.

Eventually he saw the light on in the homestead of Toussaint Trueblood, dawn yet an hour away.

When he knocked and Toussaint opened the door, he said, "I don't suppose you saw any geese on the way over and shot a couple of them to save me the trip of going out into that cold beyond?"

"I hope you have coffee on," Jake said, rubbing his hands.

Toussaint pointed to the pot atop the stove, steam curling out of its spout. Jake drank as Toussaint finished getting dressed. Slipping into a mackinaw that he pointed out had shell loops sewn into the waist which already held several double-ought buck rounds, he said, "You can use this one"—taking a pair of shotguns from the corner and holding one out to Jake.

Jake looked it over, tested its weight and balance. It was a Colt side hammer, double-barrel twelve-gauge. He put the stock up to his shoulder and looked down the long blued barrels, then took it away again and held it by the middle in one hand.

"What's that one?" he asked Toussaint, who hefted the other one as he reached for his old black felt hat.

"Thomas Horsley model. My papa gave it to me, along with a railroad watch that never did keep the right time and his old razor—about everything he owned, except for a deck of playing cards had drawings of naked women on them I lost somewhere. I cut the barrels down four inches. You know, for close-in work, case I needed it."

They drank down the hot coffee, then went out into the yawning morning. They could see the first signs the sky was turning off to the east. They rode in silence, except for the creak of their saddle leather; it was too cold and too early to carry on a conversation. A warm bed seemed about the right place to be.

They came to where Cooper's Creek cut slightly westward, then angled north in a serpentine manner and followed it for a time, then turned off through the dead grass for another ten minutes or so. Here the land rose slightly like a calcified ocean wave, then topping it they saw below the small lake sitting like an unpolished silver platter under the graying sky. Cattails bordered its edges and shifted slightly in a light northerly wind.

Toussaint led the way down to the lake and they stopped several yards short of the water's edge, dismounted, and ground-reined their mounts. Carrying their shotguns, they eased down to where the cattails were, then worked their way in among them. Toussaint said, "This seems about as good a spot as any."

"You're the expert," Jake said.

"They'll come out of the north, the way I figure it," he said, pointing. "They won't see us till they get right on top of us. They'll see that water, then they'll see the cattails but not us, not at first. Least I hope not."

Jake looked up at the sky, which had some streaks of pink growing in it. He didn't see any geese.

"That the way you heard they come, out of the north?" he said.

"Only makes sense for 'em to go south in the winter, north in the summer, like every other creature that is restless."

They squatted on their heels and waited, watched as the sky grew lighter, could see the bands of pastels, of pink and ochre, and as the sky became lighter still, the wind picked up and stirred the cattails even more and set them to knocking against one another and sent ripples over the previously mirrored surface of the lake.

"Flyway," Toussaint said.

"What?"

"It's what the goose hunters call such a place—a flyway. Because there is water for 'em to set down in and rest. I reckon they been flying like this all their lives and know every speck of water between here and Mexico. I reckon they been using these flyways for a thousand years."

"Hunting seems to turn you philosophical," Jake said.

"Just makes me wonder how they know such things," Toussaint said.

Then they heard it: the distant honk of geese.

"Hear that?" Toussaint said.

Jake nodded.

"Better get ready."

"I've been ready since last night."

"Remember, all we need are to knock down a couple of fat ones, one at least. The rest we'll let go on."

"Any particular color you'd like?" Jake said.

Toussaint grinned.

"Nah, it don't make no difference; I think they're all colored about the same anyway."

The honking grew louder.

"Must be a lot of them," Toussaint whispered. Both men had their guns aimed skyward.

Then suddenly they saw them, three groups flying close together in wavering V's, their dark bodies long and the same color gray as the sky, their necks stretched out, their black wings beating the air.

"Wait . . ." Toussaint whispered.

"You shoot, I'll shoot," Jake said.

The leading flock flew right over and kept going, as did the second. But the third wave of geese slowed and dropped down out of the sky, their wings rigid, catching air, their bodies thrusting forward at the last moment as the leaders splashed down into the water.

Toussaint leapt up and fired both barrels, even as the others were coming in for a landing. Jake followed suit.

There was a flurry of wings batting the air and the honks and cries of the geese set up the alarm for the others still airborne that swerved away from the water and lifted higher still into the sky. But it was too late for three of them. In an instant it seemed everything was over. They could hear now the distant distress of the last of them flying off.

"Thing is," Jake said, looking at the three floaters, "how are we going to retrieve them?" Toussaint was already stripping out of his clothes.

"Shit, only one way I know. You coming or are you just going to stand there and watch me drown?"

Later, riding back, the game tied to their saddle horns, Toussaint was saying, "That water shrunk my nuts to peas it was so damn cold."

They were following the curve of the creek again and it was full light now and they felt weary from the hunt and the cold swim and having gotten up early. They were thinking ahead to a warm dinner and sitting around with their stomachs full, to some hot coffee and pie.

Suddenly Jake drew his reins.

"What is it?" Toussaint said.

"You see that?" Jake was pointing at something in the water.

"Where?"

"There."

Then Toussaint saw it: the bobbing boots, the legs going into them. He saw them, then they disappeared under the water and he kept looking and they resurfaced again.

"Somebody's drowned," Toussaint said, "in that cold mean creek."

Jake dismounted and went and stood at the edge of the bank, looking down. Toussaint walked his mule over close, said, "What you thinking of doing?"

"We need to get him out."

"Yeah, that's what I thought you were thinking."

It was then that somebody finally helped Nat Pickett. But he never felt the helping hands, nor saw the faces of the men so kind, nor heard their voices as they stood over him and discoursed as to how it was most assuredly murder, with the now cut rope still trailing from his neck.

"Weighted him down with something, that's for sure. I couldn't lift it out of the mud," Toussaint said, shivering as he dressed again.

"You know this fellow?" Jake asked. "Ever seen him before?"

"No."

"Neither have I."

"Well, it's not like this territory is filled up with Negroes," Toussaint said, pulling on boots that didn't seem to want to go on easy over wet socks. "I suspect once you get him into town, somebody will know who he is."

"Yeah," Jake said. "Somebody sure should. Will you ride on back to your place and bring a wagon? I'll wait here with him."

Toussaint mounted without a word, his countenance grim. The dead man was hardly more than a boy, about the same age as his own boy, Dex, who had been shot to death a few months earlier. It was plain to see they had abused him before tossing him in the creek, whoever it was did this to him.

"What they did to him," he said as he held back the reins before heading out, "they shouldn't have done to a dog."

Jake watched him ride off at a lope.

You're right, he thought. *They shouldn't have done such a thing, whoever they were.* And when he looked at the boy's battered and blanched face, more ashen than it was brown now, the fingers curled and stiff, he felt sick and angry.

He shucked off his coat and placed it over the boy's face and torso, then waited in the cold wind, thinking about the boy and the geese he and Toussaint had shot. How they had been graceful in the air, their bodies warm, their hearts beating, their blood pumping, and then suddenly all that was taken away from them by a single act of will. Just as the dead boy's life had been taken by a willful act.

And the sky, soon enough, with the rising sun became clear and beautiful and blue.

2

⁂

JOHN SAID, "I KNOW THIS BOY."

They had Nat Pickett laid out on Tall John's undertaking table there in a room with shelves of jars whose smells were strange and trays of odd-looking instruments. No place for a young cowboy.

"Then you might tell us who he is," Jake said.

"I believe he is a hand over to Bob Parker's place, the Double Bar, but the word *was* would be more in keeping. I have seen him in the Three Aces a few times with some of the other boys from that spread. Saturday nights, usually. Name's Nat, I do believe, though I don't recall his last name. Some of the boys called him Midnight."

Toussaint stood in the corner, not caring much for the place with its odd smells, with its long wood table. He could see, on a sideboard, various-size needles and black thread, a jar with cotton in it, a brown corked bottle had a POISON label on it. He also saw a contraption and asked, "What is that thing?" The contraption was a copper cylinder with a pump handle and rubber tubes.

"Embalming machine," John said.

"I'll wait outside," Toussaint said.

John examined the wounds, the gashes on the neck and wrists, from where he had clipped the wire that bound them.

"This boy suffered brutal," he said.

"Yes, I can see that," Jake said. For, if anyone knew the determination of injuries and their result, it was the lawman who everyone knew as Jake Horn, and not as Tristan Shade, a former Denver physician.

"A quick burial is in order, considering his condition, unless you know of kin nearby?" Jake added.

John shook his head.

"I do not. Fact is, I don't know of a single other Negro within a hundred miles of here."

"Can you get him in the ground today?"

"It is Thanksgiving, Marshal."

"Not for him it isn't."

"Sure, I can get him buried today if I can find someone to help me dig a grave."

"Thanks," Jake said. "Send me over the bill when it's done."

Outside Toussaint sat atop his wagon seat, looking off toward the fallen sky, now heavy with snow clouds, the wind coming down the street sharp as knives that cut a message on the skin: a warning about the coming winter.

"I promised Karen I'd come right back," he said. "She's still a little nervous to be left alone out there, especially so now that she has the boy."

"Go on ahead," Jake said.

"You still coming to dinner?"

"Maybe later. I'm going out to Bob Parker's place to ask after that dead young man. Seems to me somebody has to know something. He didn't just end up in that creek for no reason."

"If any of them had a hand in this, do you think they'll own up to it?"

"He was one of their own for a time, maybe one of them might feel some obligation to say something if he knows anything."

"I wouldn't count on it; he wasn't really one of their own. Not really."

Jake understood the breed's meaning. He walked down to the livery where Sam Toe kept saddle horses for rent. Sam had been resting on two bales of hay, resting and dreaming fitfully about an old acquaintance: Rowdy Jeff Pine.

He and Rowdy Jeff had been partnered up a summer a few years earlier when they both worked for a big sheep rancher in Montana. They spent that summer in a high meadow full of sheep and wildflowers sprinkled like various colors of paint over the sweet flowing grass. Just the two of them and not a soul within rifle shot, as far as either could tell.

In the dream Rowdy Jeff had suddenly kissed Sam on the mouth. It brought him full awake. He sat bolt upright, spitting and sputtering, then saw standing there who he believed was Rowdy Jeff. It was hard to tell with all that hammered light behind him and floating hay dust in the air. Then, rubbing the sleep out of his eyes, Sam recognized the town marshal.

His hands shook as he saddled the horse at Jake's request.

"Are you feeling poorly?" Jake asked.

"No sir, just bad dreams that sticks with me."

Jake walked the animal Sam had saddled out of the barn and into the cold breath of the world. Sam followed him and stood watching him ride off toward the north, thinking how much that marshal looked like

Rowdy Jeff with his dark beard and long moustaches and sharp blue eyes.

It wasn't the first time since he and Rowdy Jeff split company at the end of that long summer that he'd had the dream. Sam tried to shake off the memory like a dog shaking off water he'd swum in. The loneliness of that time was a killer to Sam's spirits as he recalled the constant bleating of sheep, the skulking coyotes they'd had to stand guard against long into the black nights. Just him and Rowdy Jeff, playing cards in between and drinking skunk-tasting coffee until their brains grew numb trying to keep busy and their thoughts off women and whiskey. Rowdy Jeff telling about all the women he'd known, and not a woman within a hundred miles to relieve them. Things like that got to a man after a time.

He went and found the half-drunk bottle of rye down in the grain bin where he kept it hid and rubbed the sides of it clean before pulling the cork and taking a long swallow, trying his best to drown the memory of way back then. He'd just as soon not have to think about it ever again, but knew the dreams and thoughts of Rowdy Jeff would not leave him alone for long.

Jake rode with the image of the dead boy behind his eyelids. Nobody deserved such a fate. He rode with rising anger toward anyone who would do such a thing—one human to another. It made no sense. What happened to men to cause them to commit such acts? He'd seen much savagery in the war. But war pitted one man against another without necessarily the consent of either and made them desperate with due cause: survival. But this what they did to that boy was a pure pitiless act of the worst sort.

He rode at a steady pace, hoping to reach Bob Parker's

before the weather turned worse, for he could practically taste the snow.

The fallow grasslands had turned the color of broom brush and just as dry, spread as far as the eye could see, tan and lifeless and full of empty. Clouds tumbled in the sky. Way off to his left he could see a copse of trees, black and barren, like the charred remains of some old fort.

Bob Parker's ranch house, along with several other buildings, sat back from the road a quarter mile. In that flat country it wasn't hard to see a quarter mile. He saw woodsmoke curling out of several of the stovepipes and he turned up the trace leading to the spread.

As he drew nearer, several hands were digging a well with picks and shovels. One was leaning against a wagon, watching. They all paused what they were about when they saw him ride up. Some of them looked familiar to him, men he'd seen in town at the saloon or getting a haircut or perhaps in Otis Dollar's general store.

He rode among them, then halted his horse and looked at them in general, but specifically the one leaning against the wagon, his hands empty of pick or shovel, figuring him to be the ramrod of the crew, and said, "Anybody here know a hand named Nat? A colored man?"

He could tell by the change in their faces they knew who he spoke of. Yet their suspicion of the stranger among them kept them taciturn, except for the one leaning against the wagon, who straightened and spat.

"What about him?" the man said. His hand reaching inside his jacket, now taking out his makings for rolling a shuck. *Acting real casual*, Jake thought.

"Found him dead today."

"Dead?" a curly-headed young man holding a pick said.

"That's right," Jake said. "Somebody killed him," seeing how that would set with them.

The curly-headed youth dropped his pick, leaned and took it up again. He had the look of surprise on him. But the one making himself a smoke didn't seem at all affected by the news, nor did the other four.

"That's too bad," the cigarette smoker said, licking his cigarette into shape. "He was a fair hand, that boy."

"How'd it happen, mister?" the curly-headed one said.

"Somebody beat him, then drowned him," Jake said. "Tied him down with some sort of weight around his neck. Wanted to make sure he stayed down under the creek they threw him in. Hard way to die. Imagine dying like that."

He saw the youth blanch, saw the way his hands fussed with the pick handle.

The man leaning against the wagon twisted off the ends of his cigarette, put one end in his mouth, and struck a Lucifer off the wagon's steel rim, then cupped the flame in his hand as he lowered his cigarette to it.

Taking his sweet time, Jake thought, *perhaps to make up a story he wants to sell me.*

The man took a deep draw off the smoke, then let it out, the wind carrying the smoke away. The others looked cold and he said to them, "Somebody tell you all to take a vacation?" That set them to working on digging the well again, even the curly-headed boy whose sideburns covered his cheeks.

Then the man smoking looked at Jake and said, "What's your business in all this anyway?"

Jake turned over the flap of his coat so the man could see the badge.

"I'm the town marshal in Sweet Sorrow," he said.

"S'at so?"

Real casual like nothing fazed him, like it didn't mean anything at all that here was a lawman inquiring after the murder of one of their own. But like Toussaint Trueblood had pointed out, this Nat, this Negro, really wasn't one of their own except by occupation, maybe.

"What was his last name?" Jake said.

The smoking man grunted and turned away to watch the others digging the well, as though he hadn't heard the question. Jake walked his horse up and bumped the man nearly knocking him off his feet.

"I asked you what his last name was?"

The man regained his balance, looked like he was ready to fight, then something made him think better of it and his stance slackened, the cigarette dangling between his lips, his fists down at his sides now.

"Pickett!" the man said. "His name was Nat Pickett! Least that's what he said it was, but you know you can't never trust a nigger completely to tell you the truth about nothing. Maybe that was his real name, maybe it wasn't. It's what he said it was and around here we take a man at his word."

"What's your name?" Jake said.

Their gazes locked.

"None of your goddamn business."

"What? You think I won't find out?"

Jake saw out of the corner of his eye the others had stopped their well-digging again, had paused to watch the exchange. He stepped his horse back two steps, looked at them all.

"Somebody killed Mr. Nat Pickett," Jake announced for their benefit, fixing his gaze again on the man who'd been smoking. "I'm going to find out who it was killed him and I'm going to arrest them. That's the deal. Anybody know anything they'd be wise to tell me, otherwise maybe the wrong man gets arrested, put in jail—maybe even hanged for the murder . . ."

Then he turned his horse back up the trace toward the house and when he arrived Bob Parker was already standing out front, as though he was already aware there was trouble in the air, had somehow sensed it, and came out to meet it.

3

❖⟲❖

SOME ARE JUST BORN WITH A GIFT.

An uncle—Reese—came one fine spring day to the farm and stayed the summer helping with the harvest and slept upstairs in the hot airless loft, sharing a bed with the boy—Willy Silk, son to Reese's brother, Barth, and only child.

Willy was sixteen at the time and thought to be going off to seminary in a year or two.

Uncle Reese, on the other hand, had strayed about as far from a seminary or any sort of institution like it in his forty-odd years of wandering. Reese was referred to as the black sheep of the Silks, the prodigal son.

He said one night when it was too hot to sleep and they could almost hear the corn growing, "You ever had a woman, Willy?"

"No sir."

"But you have thought about getting you one before you go off to that seminary?"

Then there was a long silence between them and so dark and moonless one couldn't see the other, even though they shared the same bed.

"Well, you've thought about it, right?" Reese repeated, for when he was onto a subject he enjoyed he was less likely to let go of it than a dog a bone.

"Nothing wrong with thinking about it," Reese said. "Nothing wrong with doing it, either. You about come to the right age to be thinking about it. Me, I was twelve my first time I done it with a gal."

Willy liked his uncle Reese about as well as he liked anyone, for the man just seemed like adventure: All the stories Reese told him—how he'd been a sailor once, and fought in the Civil War and got caught and escaped, and how he went down to Brazil and looked for gold, and so forth. Reese even hinted he had been a river pirate and spent some time in jail in San Francisco.

"I reckon there's nothing wrong with thinking about it," Willy said wistfully.

"Hell no." Reese laughed. "God*damn* but it's terrible hot. Let's say we go sleep in the yard."

So they did and that night Reese talked to Willy about women and getting in and out of trouble and how much fun it could be as long as you didn't get caught breaking the law, but hell, laws were made to be broken and if a feller didn't break a little law now and then, he sure wasn't doing much real living. It got Willy to thinking about a future other than the seminary.

And that is how it began that it was learned Willy had a gift.

For the following afternoon after they'd hoed weeds out of half a field of upstart corn, they walked on back to a copse of trees that stood black and tall against the pewter sky to take their lunch and whilst there, Reese said, "I bet you ain't even ever shot a pistol have you, Willy?"

"No sir, but I've shot Dad's old rifle lots." Reese said it wasn't the same thing.

Then Reese took out his pistol with gutta-percha grips and said, "This is a .32 Smith & Wesson five-shooter—what some call a belly gun. See how it fits your hand."

And when Willy took hold of it like it was a deadly snake, Reese laughed and told him not to be afraid of it, said, "How's it feel?"

"Feels like trouble," Willy said, and Reese laughed so hard he fell off the log they'd been sitting on.

"Thing is," Reese said, "to be careful where you point it. Guns has been known to go off accidental. Probably been more men shot and killed accidental than on purpose. Ho, ho, ho."

"Feels real good, Uncle Reese," Willy said, as he grew used to its weight in his hand.

"Aim it yonder at that dead limb, see if you can hit it."

"That one?"

"No, that one yonder, just beyond."

It was a limb about the size around of a man's thumb, sticking up about two foot high.

"Just hold it straight out in front of you and look down the barrel like it was your finger you were pointing, then squeeze the trigger like you would a girl's titty."

Willy blushed and Reese said, "That's right. You ain't never squeezed a girl's titty, but I bet you have a cow's. Squeeze it like you was milking a cow's titty, firm but steady."

"Like this here?"

The pistol barked and that's when Reese and Willy both found out about the gift Willy had been given. That thumb limb disappeared, most of it, just a sharp piece left, white as bone where the bark had been shot away.

"Goddamn," Reese declared. "Knock the rest of it down, so I know it wasn't no accident."

And coolly Willy shot the rest of the limb away with the next shot, so there wasn't even an inch left sticking up.

"Shit, boy, you're a natural."

Willy looked like he didn't want the gun to ever leave his hand.

"You was to put that pistola down the waist of your pants you'd look just like a desperado," Reese said. Willy blushed scarlet and felt like something in him was going to burst.

That evening at supper Willy's mother—a man-sized woman—served ham smothered in red-eye gravy, a pan full of warm biscuits, sweet potatoes, and said, "I heard shooting going on this afternoon. You two know anything about that?"

"I was taking some target practice out in them woods of yours yonder, Ethel," Reese said.

Ethel Silk never cared much for Reese's sort and would not have tolerated him in her house had he not been Barth's brother. She thought him footloose and irresponsible, a man who figured to get by on his charm and handsome looks, a sweet talker and a rogue. And she wouldn't have had him around even then, except the weeds in the corn was growing wild and the roof was leaking and about ten hundred other things needed fixing when he showed up out of the blue. So she let him stay on, thinking at least till most of the man work got caught up on.

"I don't want you firing guns around Willy," she said. "One of those bullets could ricochet . . ."

Willy started to confess the truth, that it was him doing the shooting, but Reese gave him a look that warned he'd be better off not owning up to something like that unless forced.

"A man packing a gun might as well be carrying a lit stick of dynamite for all the trouble it will bring him," she said. "I don't want you getting any notions in your head, Willy. You tell him, Reese."

"Tell him what, Ethel?"

"About what sorts of trouble a man with a gun can get himself into."

"You listen to your ma, Willy," Reese said. "And pass them sweet taters if you don't mind."

It was the Fourth of July and Willy's daddy had been dead close to a year already. That night they all went into Hopewell to watch the fireworks display and eat ice cream and for the first time in a long time, Willy could see his ma was in a good mood and it made him feel good that she was; she'd been real down in the mouth ever since his pa had died. And later when they all came home again, Reese cracking jokes in the wagon on the ride back, his ma laughed aloud and said, "Oh, stop it, Reese, you're making my sides ache." And once they got there, Reese told Willy he reckoned he'd stay up for a time and for Willy to go on to bed. A summer rainstorm rushed in and cooled everything down to a pleasantness that allowed Willy to sleep in the upstairs room and he fell asleep fast enough only to be awoken sometime later by the crash of thunder.

"Reese?" he said, sitting up in the dark. Then flashes of light from the storm filled the room and he could see the room was empty. "Reese?"

He thought he'd go and look for Reese, see if he was drunk maybe and sitting out in the rain, perhaps asleep out there on his back in the yard, as he'd found him once before, his mouth open with the rain filling it up.

He tugged on his drawers and went down looking for

Reese, went out and stood on the porch, the rain falling so hard it sounded like water boiling.

"Reese?" he said, calling out his name just loud enough to be heard over the rushing rain. "Reese?"

But he didn't see a trace of Reese in the lightning flashes: not sitting there on the porch or lying out in the yard, or nowhere else. It just didn't feel right somehow, but wasn't nothing he could do about it. Maybe Reese had taken off, left for parts unknown. He could have gone off with as little notice as he had arrived; it was Reese's way.

Willy felt abandoned at the thought that Reese had left.

He waited a time there on the porch, hoping maybe he'd see Reese coming through the rain, thinking it possible he had gone to the barn to check on the horses or out to the privy. But there wasn't any sign of him and after a time Willy went back inside the house and started up the stairs. Then he heard something coming from his mother's room, a conversation—muted beyond the door. He stopped and put his ear to the door and listened and realized who it was talking. His heart sank.

He went on up the stairs to his loft and listened to the rain and tried not to think about what he'd heard downstairs. Tried not to think about what Reese and his mother were doing. It seemed unthinkable to him she would let Reese in her room, the way she was so openly scornful of him. The air seemed charged with something that caused the hair on his arms to stand up and made sleep hard to come by.

The next day when he saw the two of them sitting at the kitchen table, drinking coffee, empty plates before them, not speaking or even looking at each other, he didn't say anything, just went about as usual, as though he didn't know anything about the way the two of them were acting. But later, when he saw them heading off to the woods together, he went in and found Reese's pistol and took the money he knew she kept in a cigar box on the top shelf of the closet above her dresses with the scent of potpourri and cedar. He put the money and a few clothes in a satchel, went out to the barn, put a halter on the work horse, and rode away bareback and grim.

By the time Willy made it to Cincinnati, he was about starved and used up, save for two dollars in his shoe. If it hadn't been for the poster and his ability to read, he might well have ended up jumping into the Ohio River, just another victim of life's failure. He'd stood on the bridge and looked down into that muddy swirling water and saw it as a quick way out of a mean life. The water swirled gentle, like it was inviting him. It was a long jump. He figured with luck he'd break his neck and save himself the sorrow of drowning.

Then he saw the poster tacked there on a crosstie and it read like fate had written it:

SHOOTING MATCH • SATURDAY, JULY 10TH
FAIRGROUNDS
ALL ARE INVITED
ONE DOLLAR ENTRY FEE
SINGLE ELIMINATION
11 A.M. SHARP!
$50 Grand Prize

Colonel Ben Lily never saw such a goddamn pistol shooter in his entire life. Skinny kid in high-water pants and rough brogans. Straight off the farm, he reckoned. Hayseed and bumpkin combined. But *jaysus god* the kid could shoot! And when Willy won the first-place prize money, he didn't know quite what it meant, whether it was luck or something else. It was more money than he'd ever seen, except in a bank once.

A man in a big fancy hat and butter soft-fringed jacket decorated in quills and bright beadwork approached him and said, "My name's Colonel Ben Lily, son, and I'd like to make your acquaintance and offer you a job with my Wild West Combination." That's how it started, Willy Silk's professional shooting career—billed as part of Colonel Ben Lily's Wild West Combination: **Willy Silk—The Cincinnati Kid—Boy Pistoleer. Come One, Come All!**

And to sell the thing to the public and make a little extra, Colonel Lily included at every stop in the tour a shooting match offering: **One Hundred Dollars to Any Man Who Can Out Shoot the Pistoleer! Ten-dollar entry fee!**

Nobody did in a year, though one man, an old fellow with a burnt face, came close, shooting forty-seven of fifty glass balls, but Willy shattered them all. And with his growing reputation came the growing adoration of fans—women fans notwithstanding and most especially—and Willy Silk soon understood the pleasures Uncle Reese had talked about those long hot Ohio nights back on the farm—the power a woman carries in her body.

But with the women came the whiskey, too.

And liquor was a snake that once it bit you left its poison in your blood in a way you liked and the way that helped steal your own power like a thief, stealing your good sense and resolve.

By years two and three and four, Willy had begun to fail with regularity the shooting of every glass ball or every bird tied to a stake, and six times lost shooting matches to men who came out of the crowd—one a goddamn farmer, like himself, or like what himself had once been. It was a boy with one blue eye and one brown who said, "My name's Gerald and glad to meet'cha, Mr. Kid," then commenced to shatter every glass ball—all fifty—in a row while Willy missed four and Colonel Lily once more laid out a hundred dollars cash to a grinning hayseed.

"Son, I gotta tell you," Colonel Lily said one evening toward the end of the fourth season there in Willy's tent. "What you was when I first seen you, you ain't no more. Don't know if it's the whiskey or the cooze or a combination of the two, but either can and will ruin a man, and the two together is like sticking a fork in your eye and cutting off your nuts—leaves you about useless to me, and I'm going to have to terminate our relationship, don't you see."

By this time Willy had learned to cuss as well and said, "Fuck I need you for old man? I can hire on with any number of combinations, Buffalo Bill's included. Fuck I need you for?"

And that was it, his candle flame blown out—or so it seemed.

Willy set loose on his own, found the going a lot rougher than he'd imagined, thought twice about returning to the farm, but pride wouldn't allow it. He heard, too, Reese had married his mother, then stole her blind before abandoning her, and she had to put the farm up for sale. He did not know how much was true, how much wasn't. Whiskey made him not care.

A big match in Denver drew his attention. Put on by a rich man who they said didn't have nothing better to do than entertain himself, a man who featured himself as fine a pistoleer as could be found on either side of the Atlantic Ocean. An Englishman named Tidwell.

Willy took the train from El Paso to Denver, leaving behind a woman named Lucy who had kept him in fine shirts and fresh cigars by doing what she was best at: selling herself to men—though Willy was special and got it free as long as he professed his love for her, which he did clear up until the day he boarded the north-bound without so much as leaving Lucy a note of farewell.

In the audience that day was one Quincy Adams Shaw, bereaved father of Tecumseh Shaw, murdered, he was convinced, by a man named Tristan Shade who had fled the scene. The bereaved man had previously hired a private detective—one Prince Puckett—to locate and bring about justice, or revenge, whichever came first. But said Puckett had disappeared off the face of the earth—dead himself, figured the elder Shaw, probably by the same hand that had killed his son.

And so Mr. Quincy Adams Shaw was drawn to the highly touted shooting match in hopes of finding a new *man* most handy with firearms to see the job the missing Puckett had begun completed.

Willy Silk didn't give a shit about what other men might want of him.

Life had boiled down to one thing—money, what it could buy.

He'd become hard as the old trees behind the cornfields he once hoed weeds out of with his uncle Reese. Just as hard and black inside.

The match begun in a light rain.

It soon enough got down to just Willy and the Englishman, who used a set of custom silver pistols with staghorn grips. Son of a bitch could fire with either hand

and nearly equally as well. Willy sweated under his stained Stetson, thinking it might be just one more match he'd lose in a long series of losing lately.

The Englishman shot forty-nine in a row. But a raindrop fell into his shooting eye just as he fired at and missed number fifty. Smiled like the cat that ate the canary, knowing hardly any man but himself could hit them all in a light rain turning harder by the minute.

Willy shot them down like ducks he wanted to eat for supper, forty-six, forty-seven, forty-eight, forty-nine—reloading in between—then took his sweet time, knowing the worst he could do was tie the Englishman, the rain like a curtain of silver threads between himself and the target.

Quincy Adams Shaw looked on with rapt interest, knowing he would offer the winner whatever money it would take to find one man and shoot him like a glass ball.

The Englishman stood aside, watching, too, his soft gray bowler speckled dark from raindrops, looking confident. Thinking: *You bloody Americans . . .*

Willy thumbed back the hammer on his nickel-plated Mervin & Hulbert .44-.40. *It feels good, Uncle Reese*, he thought bitterly.

The sounds of the shot and that of the glass ball breaking were as one.

Shards of glass sprinkled the wet air like a handful of tossed diamonds. The crowd let out a collective breath, then applause.

"Most extraordinary," was all the Englishman said. "We shall have to do it again sometime."

Willy holstered the piece, its barrel hot to the touch, held out his hand for the prize money, then pocketed it and went off to the nearest saloon, where Quincy Adams Shaw found him.

"Can I buy you a whiskey?"

Willy said, without looking up, "Sure, why the hell not."

4

BOB PARKER WAS LARGE and thick as a slab of beef. But the thing you noticed most about him was his eyebrows. They looked like a set of thorn bushes riding the ridge of his brow; thick and wiry, untrimmed.

"Marshal," he said by way of greeting before Jake could even bring his horse to a complete stop. "What brings you this way on such a brittle day?" His gaze went from Jake to scouring the threatening sky.

"Gone snow," he said. "I can feel it in my feet."

"One of your hands, a young colored man named Nat Pickett," Jake said. "Found him dead earlier."

He saw the scowl creep over that big pan face, the eyebrows bunch.

"Dead? Dead of what?"

"Murdered," Jake said.

Bob looked off, up the trace to where the men were digging a new well. One of the old ones had gone dry. There were four on the spread. Wind brushed the grass down flat, then let it up again and brushed it down flat again.

"Murdered you say? You know this for a fact?"

"Found him at the bottom of Cooper's Creek, bound and trussed like some poor animal. He had a rope around his neck, weighted down, but by what exactly I couldn't say. Was hard enough to get him cut free. He was beaten pretty bad, too."

Bob took a deep draw of the cold air and exhaled slowly.

"I'm a son of a bitch," he said. "Don't know why anybody would want to kill that boy. He was a good hand, knew horses, knew cows, too."

"What can you tell me about him?"

"You mean like where is he from?"

"That too."

"Down south from somewhere—like most, all over. Think I heard him mention Oklahoma once."

"He have any family you know of, somebody I could write to and tell them he's dead?"

The rancher shrugged his broad slopping shoulders.

"Don't get into the hired help's business too much. They come and they go—like the wind, most of 'em. Maybe you should ask one of them yonder digging that well."

"I did but that didn't get me anywhere."

"Yeah, they're a tight-lipped bunch. Some of 'em is souther'n boys; always knew them souther'n boys to be tight-lipped. You ask Tig?"

"Which one is he?"

The rancher pointed toward them and said, "That curly-headed boy. I think him and Nat was close, but I couldn't say for sure. I seen 'em riding off toward town together sometimes."

"I'd like to take Pickett's personal things, see if I can't locate a relative and send them on," Jake said.

"Sure, I can understand that," Bob said and stepped

off the porch and walked toward the long low building that was the bunkhouse and showed Jake which bunk was the colored boy's. Underneath there lay a soogins rolled up and tied and Jake pulled it out and set it on the bunk and untied it and rolled it open.

A blue shirt. Razor, razor strap, pair of dungarees hardly worn, almost new, two pairs of socks, one that needed darning, a copper-framed tintype of a group of colored folks looked like they were standing in front of a church. One bone-handled knife in a sheath. *He could have used that,* Jake thought. A bird's-eye-handled Colt revolver. *He could have used that, too.* No wallet. Jake made a mental note to ask the undertaker if he'd found any possessions in the clothing the boy was wearing.

"That's it . . ." Bob said. "Not much to show, but then none of them boys would have, always drifting from job to job like they are wont to do."

Jake rolled everything back up again, tied the end strings together and carried it out again and settled it across the pommel of his saddle.

"What'd you do with him?" Bob asked. "Nat's body?"

"Tall John is probably burying him as we speak—there in the cemetery just outside of town."

"Wait a minute," the rancher said and went into the house and came out again a few minutes later and handed Jake a twenty-dollar double eagle. "If it comes to more than that, let me know. He wasn't due his pay till end of month, but considering the circumstance . . ."

Jake pocketed the coin. Wind ruffled the horse's mane. The sky sat about as low as a man standing now and there was a strange sound to the wind.

"I'm sorry to hear of such a tragedy on a day meant to give Thanks," Bob said. "You're welcome to stay to dinner."

"Got a long ride back," Jake said. "Best I get going."

Bob offered Jake his hand and Jake shook it, then forked his horse and turned it back toward town. He judged it to be about midday.

He dropped off Nat Pickett's personal effects at the jail, then rode over to the livery.

Sam Toe was clearly drunk, almost too much so to stand.

"Here's to turkey and all the trimmings," Sam said in a salubrious salute, holding the nearly empty second bottle he'd worked on that day. "Happy Thanksgiving, Marshal."

Jake traded him out the horse for a wagon with a team and together they got the team hitched to it, Sam mumbling the same name over again like a curse: "Rowdy Jeff. Rowdy Jeff . . ." Jake didn't know what he was talking about, but didn't much care either.

He picked up Clara and the girls. Clara had baked a gooseberry pie to take along.

"You look worried about something," she said when they'd gone a few miles in silence.

Jake didn't want to tell her about the drowned boy, especially not in front of the girls.

"The weather," he lied. "Might come a hard snow the way everybody's talking. If it does, we might be stuck out there at Toussaint's overnight."

Clara nudged a little closer to Jake on the wagon seat and said, "That's wouldn't be so bad, would it?"

He looked over at her, saw that sweet smile she had a way of giving, and he said, "No, I reckon it wouldn't."

"You sure that's all that's bothering you?"

He looked back over his shoulders at the girls, who

were busy playing some sort of game with each other, chattering like squirrels.

"Nothing I can talk about in front of them," he said.

"I understand."

The road had hardened with the cold and old ruts frozen over made for a bumpy ride. A mile or so out, they saw some pronghorns off in the distance looking at them in between grazing on the last of the grasses.

Clara said, "Thank you for inviting us to go along, Jake," and placed a gloved hand over his holding the reins. It was a gesture that endeared him to her. It did not escape him that the feeling he had toward them all was one of *family*. To a stranger they would simply seem like a man and his wife and children traveling the road from one place to another. He liked the idea.

Toussaint came to the door and motioned them all inside. Little Stephen's eyes brightened at the sight of the girls and Clara and Karen kissed cheeks, then everyone removed their coats, Toussaint taking them to the mud room to hang them on brass hooks. The place smelled of warm food and a fire crackled in the fireplace.

The children went off to Stephen's room and Clara pitched in to give Karen a hand with the meal. Jake motioned Toussaint to step out onto the porch and they did without bothering to put on their coats.

"You say anything to Karen about what we found?"

"No, not yet I didn't. Figured this wasn't the day for it. When I came back for the wagon, I just told her it was something you needed me to help you with. You say anything to Clara?"

"No, and I don't want to either."

"They don't need to know such things," Toussaint

said. "Troubling things like that. You find out anything out to Bob's?"

"Nothing much, last name is about all. Pickett," Jake said. "That was his name, Nat Pickett."

It began to snow.

"Pickett, huh."

"Yeah."

Jake saw Toussaint looking off toward the lone gravestone where his son lay buried. *The Negro boy would have been about the same age,* Jake reasoned. *Maybe a little older, but close enough to dredge up memories.*

"Bob say anything, about what sort of person he was, that colored boy?"

"Said he was a good hand."

"Nothing bad about him, that he was the sort to get into trouble, maybe did something to bring on a fight and that's why they killed him like they did?"

"No, he didn't say anything along those lines."

Toussaint nodded, still looking at the gravestone.

"You know of any sort of trouble a man could get himself into to have someone beat him like that and do him the way they did?" Jake said.

"No."

"Me either."

Karen came to the door and said, "Supper's on."

"We'll be in in a second," Toussaint said.

She looked at him for a long moment, then closed the door.

Stems of grass rushed along before the stiff wind, mixed with the snow, and oddly enough there was a split in the clouds way out to the west and a shaft of golden light sliced down through and touched the ground and it seemed to Jake a man could go and stand in that light and be somehow blessed and free of anything bad happening to him. But just as quick the clouds drew closed again, cutting off the light and the whole sky became dreary once more, except for the soft swirling flakes of snow.

"You think you can find them who did it?" Toussaint asked, turning his gaze away from the headstone to meet Jake's.

"I don't know if I can, but I'm sure as hell going to try."

"I was just wondering if somewhere right now that boy's people are sitting down to a table full of hot food, feeling happy and content they have each other to sit down with, and wondering, maybe, 'Where is he and what's he doing?' You think that's possible?"

"Sure, more than possible."

"Better then they don't know. At least not today."

Jake clapped Toussaint on the shoulder and said, "Let's go eat and try not to think anymore about it for now."

But all through that meal, the happy talk and the laughter, the stories Karen told on Toussaint, and the giggles of the children, the sweet way Clara smiled at him, Jake could not completely forget about Nat Pickett.

And snow, small and hard beads of it, pecked at the windows while the wind moaned and it was like a choir of sadness, a prairie song written for the lonely and lost among them.

5

SNOW SEVERAL INCHES DEEP lay over everything. Dawn broke cold as iron and the kid shook himself out of his blankets, pulled on his boots, and trudged to the privy, his boots crunching in the snow. All night long his mind fretted about Nat, what that lawman said had happened to him. *Nat was a good old boy,* Tig kept telling himself, the morning air clamping down on his bare head and hands like something with teeth.

He got inside the privy and closed the door and latched it and sat there in the dark with the light coming through the cracks. He could see his breath. It looked like he was smoking a cigarette. Sat there cold and miserable, trying to go and thinking about poor Nat.

What'd they have to go and kill him for?

But truth was, he already knew why.

God*damn* but it's cold. He shivered trying to get finished up. He had thought about it and thought about it and figured it was only the right thing to do: to ride into town and see that marshal and tell him what he knowed about Nat and why they killed him. But it would mean turning on the others, and if they knowed he was even thinking about it, he'd end up like poor Nat, only maybe at the bottom of that well they were digging and not some creek.

He finished up and pulled up his drawers and peeked out through one of the cracks toward the bunkhouse. Some of the others had come out of the bunkhouse and were trudging off toward the back kitchen of the main house where Hector fed them, pausing only long enough to give the pump handle a pump or two, in order to draw water to splash over their sleepy faces and string through their hair. He saw Taylor and Harvey and Lon, but he didn't see the other two: Dallas and Perk. Perk was like Dallas's shadow. Perk would jump through fire if Dallas told him to. Hell, he'd jump *into* fire if Dallas told him.

God*damn*, oh, god*damn*.

He waited until they went into the kitchen, then saw Dallas and Perk coming out of the bunkhouse, walking off just a ways to piss in the snow; too lazy to walk all the way to the privy. Bob had warned them not to be pissing in the snow, said more than once to them: "My woman might look out that window some morning and see you boys holding your peppers, and I sure as hell don't want her to see nothing of that sort of thing, so do your business in the privy, like civilized folks." But they no more listened to half of what Bob said than they did to each other, except for Dallas. Dallas was the leader, even though nobody appointed him anything, even though Mr. Parker, who they all called the boss, didn't pay him a dime more than the others. He won the leadership with his fists and his quick temper. Would fight to the death anyone who dared challenge him. It was rumored he had killed several men down in New Mexico. Tig didn't doubt any of the rumors; some men just had a way of putting cold fear in you and Dallas Fry was one of them.

Tig thought about what poor Nat must have went

through those final minutes of his life, surrounded by those sons a bitches, knowing he was going to die at their hands. And Dallas and them would do it slow. They'd make it hurt.

Tig waited until Dallas and Perk finished their business and headed for the kitchen without even bothering to wash their hands. He swung the door open and the cold stung his skin as he stepped lively, the dry crunch of his boots in the snow following him as he went. He jacked the pump handle until water came rushing out and splashed it over his face. He dried off with the towel tied there and went on into the kitchen, acting normal, and took a seat at the table and waited for Hector to bring him a plate. He reached for the coffee pot and saw some of the others looking at him, Dallas most especially.

"You ain't said nothing since yesterday," Dallas said. Dallas had those dark mean eyes that looked like they were going to pop out of his head any second.

"What you want me to say?"

"You and that nigger was close. Surprised you ain't had nothing to say about him getting himself killed. Why is that?"

"I don't know nothing to say about it," Tig replied. "We wan't that close."

"Sure you was. Two of you all the time going into town Saturday nights together. Getting drunk together. Screwing whores together." He saw the way Dallas was grinning now, the others grinning with him, only it wasn't the type of grinning happy men or teasing men will do. It was evil grinning.

Tig poured himself a cup of coffee, trying his level best to keep his hands steady and said, "Sure, we went into town a few times together, what of it?"

"Just was it my friend, I'd have something to say about

him getting killed, is all. I'd want to know who done it and take out my revenge on him who did."

"Well, it ain't none of my business who done it, now, is it? I mean I ain't no law or nothing. Sure I feel poorly to hear of it, but what can I do about it?"

Tig purposely put a little edge in his voice to keep out the sound of fear. He felt twice as bad now, having denied his friendship with Nat.

"No, I guess it ain't nothing you can do about it . . . Goddamn it, Hector, where the hell is my grub?"

Hector, like most ranch cookies, was a former top hand himself, bronc breaker, and all-around hand. But time and horses had busted him up and worn him down. In his younger days he might have killed a man for cursing him like Dallas did. He served up Dallas's plate without comment, then the others. The whole time a lit cigarette dangled from his lips with the smoke of it lifting into his squinting eyes.

They ate in silence, except for the scraping of forks on the plates, the slurping down of coffee, the scrape of their chairs on the floor.

Tig ate more quickly than usual this morning. And when he stood up to leave, Dallas said, "Where the hell-fire you going in such a hurry?"

"Got a bad tooth been aching me all damn night. I'm gone ride into town and see if the dentist will pull it." Then to add to the ruse, he rubbed his jaw and winced.

"Shit, old Perk'll pull that damn tooth for you. Why spend the three dollars? You'll pull Tig's tooth, won't you, Perk?"

Perk looked up from his plate. You could never tell which eye the man was looking at you with; one was his bad one and one his good, or maybe they were both good; it was hard to say because they each looked off in different directions. Nobody knew for sure which eye to look at when talking to him and nobody dared ask because Perk was touchy about the subject of his eyes. He had once beat a whore half to death because she asked him about them: what made them so damn crooked like that, was he knocked in the head as a child, or dropped or something?

One of his eyes settled on Tig, the other was sort of still staring at his plate.

"Sure, I'll pull that son bitch, just let me finish and get my plars."

Some of the others snorted.

"No thanks, I'd just as soon have a professional dentist messing with my teeth than have you pull it with your pliers."

"Well, go on then, damn you," Dallas said sourly.

Tig saddled his piebald mare and rode away without looking back. They found out what he was really up to . . . Hell, he didn't even want to think about if they found out.

First light Jake opened his eyes. Clara was asleep beside him.

She'd invited him to spend the night again after they'd returned from Toussaint and Karen's. It was late and pitch-dark and colder than a steel bolt. Jake had walked her and the girls to the door and she said, "Why don't you come in for a toddy?" He consented and waited until she got the girls settled into their beds.

They sat on the divan together and drank their toddies and listened to the fire crackle in the fireplace and once he looked over at her and saw the way the light danced in her eyes, for it was the only light in the parlor. She looked at him shyly.

"It was a lovely evening," she said.

Then she was kissing him and he was kissing her back and at some point she took him by the hand and led him back to her bedroom. The full moon cast enough ghost light into the room they didn't need a lamp to see by. He sat on the edge of the bed and watched as she began to unbutton her dress, the moon's light upon her, and he said, "Come over here."

And when she did he stood and finished the job of undoing the buttons and let the dress fall to the floor with a whisper.

"Are you sure you want to try this again?" he said.

"Yes," she said. "How about you?"

"No, I'm not . . . But then I'm not sure I *don't* want to, either."

Her hands were already working at the buttons of his shirt and she said softly, "We can weigh the morality of this thing to death, or we can simply let it be . . ."

He could feel her warmth and he wanted that warmth for his own, but the memory of another woman came to him and he was hesitant because of it. She sensed his mood, his inner conflict, and soothed him with her kisses, made whatever it was vanish with her caresses as they slipped under the heavy quilt, nestling and nuzzling until all doubt and concerns fell away.

Later she whispered his name, "Jake . . ." Then, "The girls . . ."

He rose quietly there in the still predawn dark, the room grown cold, the bed with Clara in it a warm temptation to return to; he dressed quickly, quietly, then left.

The snow that had fallen during the night, the snow that they did not hear, lay everywhere and for once the town looked beautiful and bucolic, like something an artist might paint in depicting a frontier town in winter, he thought. He felt famished in spite of the large supper he'd eaten at Toussaint's. He felt something else, too: contentment. A thing that he'd not felt in a very long time. He walked up toward the center of town and found the light on in the Fat Duck Café and went in and took the table by the window. And as he sat having his breakfast, he thought of Clara and what she meant to him. Thing was, no matter how he felt about her, he told himself, it wouldn't be fair to get her too involved with him. He was still wanted by the law and any day somebody could arrive to arrest him, or another assassin could be sent to kill him. He couldn't let Clara get in the middle of a thing like that.

He finished up his meal, gulping down a last swallow of coffee to brace himself against the cold, and walked over to the small one cell jail with its office and started a fire in the potbelly. Gus Boone, the part-time jailer, was asleep on the jail cot. He sat up when Jake rattled the door to the potbelly and rubbed the sleep out of his eyes.

"Don't you have a home to go home to?" Jake asked.

Gus coughed once, then stood.

"Got one, but sometimes I don't go there."

"Why is that?"

"Sometimes me and the old woman I live with have a falling out and I sleep here."

Jake shrugged, looked out the window. The sun was breaking over the horizon now and lighting up the snow, causing it to sparkle where the sun struck it.

"I helped old John dig a grave yesterday and I'm stiff in my shoulders," Gus said, working his shoulders, trying to work the soreness out of them. "We buried that colored boy and it was Thanksgiving, too. That's why my old woman and me fell out: me digging a grave on Thanksgiving. Said, 'Why do you have to dig a grave on such a day?' I said, 'It's money is why.' Well, it just went south from there—the whole conversation. So I took the two dollars John paid me and went to the Three Aces and drank my supper, then come here and spent the night."

Gus stood up and wrapped the blanket around his shoulders and moved over to the stove, holding out his hands to warm them and gazing toward the window, the street beyond.

"I guess I should go on home and see how she is this morning," Gus said.

Then the door rattled open and the curly-headed hand Jake encountered the previous day at Bob's walked in, stomping snow off his boots.

"Don't mean to make a mess," he said, looking at Jake.

"You came here to tell me something about Nat Pickett," Jake said.

The boy's eyes widened.

"How'd you know?"

"No other reason for you to be here."

The boy looked at Gus and didn't say anything.

Jake said to Gus, "Go on over to the café and get yourself some breakfast."

Gus looked sheepish.

"What?" Jake said.

"Got no money," Gus said.

Jake reached in his pocket and took out a dollar. Gus looked grateful. Jake said, "That's for food, not whiskey." Gus said, "Hell, I know it."

And when he left, Jake turned to the boy.

"I'm waiting."

"Nat . . . He was sort of a friend . . . I feel bad about what happened to him . . ."

Jake saw the fret.

"Who killed him and why, is all I need to know, son."

"There's this girl . . ."

6

❖ ⟡ ❖

"I WATCHED YOU OUTSHOOT the Englishman today,"
Shaw said. The man looked to Willy Silk like a judge
or banker with his Prince Albert coat, sateen cravat, and
diamond stickpin.

"So'd a lot of people," Willy said, wondering why the
man was buying him whiskies. Queerfish maybe. Willy
had met such a man in Chicago—a dandy son of a bitch
who mistook Willy for his own kind until Willy set him
straight by breaking his nose with the barrel of his pistol
and a few of his teeth too in an alley that stank of week-
old garbage and human piss.

"I could use a man of your skills," the banker or
judge said.

"Mister, let me get something straight between us—I
ain't no queerfish."

The man held up both palms defensively.

"Is this what you think I'm about, sir?"

"I don't put nothing past nobody. So if that's your
game, you been fair-warned."

"Believe me, young man, I've no interest in you in
that way."

Willy waited until the man ordered him another

whiskey and sipped the fire that warmed the blood and soothed the demons.

"And what way is it that you *are* interested in me then?"

The banker or judge or whatever he was looked about and said, "Let's retire to that table where I might speak in private with you."

"Bring along a bottle to keep us company," Willy Silk said.

Quincy Adams Shaw thought a man who was a slave to liquor, as it seemed the young shootist was, might prove an empty vessel in the long run, but he was willing to take the chance in order to get revenge for his murdered son. He bought a bottle of the house's best and followed the youth to the empty table that stood in the far and lonely corner of the saloon.

It was by now midafternoon and raining quite hard outside, which only added to the air of gloom.

Willy'd had a dream the night before that he had murdered his uncle Reese and climbed into bed with his mother. He awoke in a night sweat that neither liquor nor the nameless woman he'd picked up could alleviate and some of the dream still plagued him.

Willy waited, unsettled, for the stranger to state his business, for he did not care for the company of strangers, except for those who wore skirts. He noticed the dandy had smooth hands and wore a signet ring on one finger when the hand gripped the liquor bottle.

"I've a money proposal for you," the man said finally.

"I'm all ears," Willy said, figuring to hear the fool out, then ride on to Cheyenne, where he heard there was another big shooting match.

So Shaw laid it out for him, quick and clean as a razor cut.

Then when the dandy stopped talking, Willy said, "Kill a man, that's what you want to pay me to do?"

"Yes, exactly" came the simple reply.

"A thousand dollars, just to plug somebody?"

"Simple as that."

Willy sneered.

"Nothing simple about killing a man," Willy said. "I could hang if caught."

"May I ask if you ever have shot anyone for money or otherwise?"

"You can ask any goddamn thing you like, don't mean I'm gone answer it. What's my business is my business. You ever fuck a horse?"

Willy saw the dandy blanch, knew he wasn't used to such crude talk, didn't care.

"Point well taken," the dandy said. "Will you do it?"

"Details," Willy said.

So Quincy Adams Shaw told the youth what there was to know—how his son had been murdered by a man who'd violated the man's wife and then escaped and so on and so forth, embellishing the facts and details, bending and shaping the story into a bowl of sympathy for justice unserved and a life of promise snuffed out.

"I reckon was I to agree to this, you're aiming to tell me how I'd find your boy's killer?" Willy said. "It's a damn big country."

Here is where the man shrugged, said, "Last word I received he's somewhere in the northern territory of Dakota. I confess you aren't the first man I hired."

"What happened to the other one?"

"I don't know. After receiving word he was in a place called Bismarck and heading north, I never heard from him again. Dead, I assume, or quit."

"So maybe this killer of your son killed your hired man, too, is that it?"

"I won't lie to you—it well could be the situation."

"I'm not in the killing business, mister," Willy said, deciding a thousand dollars was just a lot of one-dollar bills stacked up together, and what would he have once he spent the money but the same as what he already had and possibly the law down on his neck to boot.

"How much would it take to get you to do it?"

"Now we're getting down to brass tacks."

They drank some more before striking a bargain— travel expenses, of course included. And that night Willy found himself a whore, surprisingly old. Why he chose her above the younger ones, he could only guess: She looked somewhat like his ma and he was feeling mean-spirited.

"What's your name?" he asked the woman once they were back in his room.

"Ruth," she said.

"Ain't you a little long in the tooth for this business, Ruth?"

"It's what I've done all my life. I don't know no other way. With age comes experience. Most want 'em young— I think because they lust after their daughters . . . But some prefer a woman with experience to teach them the ways a woman likes. Mostly the young ones like yourself. Or maybe its just some sort of fancy they get in their heads—wondering what it's like to be with an older woman. It's always the old wanting the young and the young wanting the old in this business."

Willy swallowed hard, took off his boots, fell back on the bed, and watched Ruth undress and there was something abhorrent in watching her.

She smiled and draped her bloomers over the end of the bed and came to him wearing only her stockings and leaned over him and kissed him on the mouth. She smelled like dead flowers, a cloying disturbing smell that should have put him off to her but ended up having the opposite effect.

"You think they's something wrong with me, being young and wanting you 'cause you're old?"

"What's it matter what I think, young master?" she said and kissed him again in such a soft and tender way. He closed his eyes and let happen what was to happen and for the shortest moments, he felt safe in the midnight of his soul.

And when the first beams of morning light pierced the windows of his room, he looked about and saw that she was gone and only the scent of her remained near to him. Her scent and his memory of her soft and ample flesh, how warm it was.

He went and heaved into a corner of the room, then dressed and left out of that place, bought a train ticket north from the down payment in his pocket to kill a man—something he'd never done before, but he was down to desperation, it seemed, in all phases of his young life.

He never expected to encounter his uncle Reese in Cheyenne, but that is where he found him, swamping out a gambling den, looking wasted, his hair down to past his shoulders and gone almost completely white.

He waited till dawn the next day to confront him on the street outside, put the muzzle of his pistol up hard against Reese's jaw, and said, "Move into that alley or I'll kill you right here if that is what you want."

"Willy," said Reese, once he recognized who it was assaulting him.

"I ought to just blow your fucking head off," Willy said.

"Oh hell, Willy, go ahead if that is what you want." Reese began to weep and fell to his knees and looked pathetic, like a penitent, a sinner waiting for God to either forgive him or strike him dead.

"You sure ought to do just that very thing, Willy, for I did you and your mama wrong, I'll admit. Go on and pull that trigger and shoot me . . . I got no reason to live no how. I'm just skating on borrowed time as it is."

Willy thumbed back the hammer of his pistol and Reese didn't even bother to look up.

"I ain't afraid of dying, Willy. What I'm afraid of is living."

Willy brought the gun down close to Reese's sweaty skin, there just above the brows.

"I ought to, Reese, I mean, what I heard is you cleaned Mother out of everything she had."

Reese shook his head back and forth like a hamstrung steer in agony.

"I admit to it, but it wasn't all as one-sided a thing as you might have heard. Still, that ain't no excuse for the things I done."

"You goddamn right, it ain't."

"Please, Willy, just pull the trigger and get it over and leave me here like the garbage. It's a proper place for a man like me to die . . ."

"What happened to you, Reese? You used to be somebody I looked up to, now you just look all used up. You look just like some old bum."

"I got the disease, Willy. I got the disease they call pox and it's eating me up, and the doc says it will eat up my brain, too. It's all just a matter of time, Willy. I'd just as soon not go that way. Pussy ruined me, Willy. Pussy and all the things a man will do to get it."

"Jesus Christ, Reese, I don't want to hear nothing about it."

"Shit, boy, shoot me if you got an ounce of compassion in you."

But instead Willy holstered the gun, said, "Get up, Reese, you're like some goddamn mangy dog somebody's kicked. I can't stand to see you this way."

It took a long minute for Reese to rise to his feet.

"What you gone do, Willy, if not shoot me?"

"First I'm gone get you cleaned up, then I don't know. Put you on a train to somewhere maybe. Hell, Reese, I don't know."

Reese stood there shaking like a dog come out of a cold river.

"Jesus, Reese."

They had breakfast after Willy took Reese to the local bath house run by a pair of Chinamen and paid them to trim his hair and had one of them run and buy Reese some new clothes, telling the Chinamen to burn his old ones.

They ate in a restaurant full of good smells and Willy watched his uncle eat like he was starved—which he was—his hands shaking hard enough he had to keep forking up his eggs again and again.

Reese ran over his history as he ate, telling Willy about how he come to get involved with Willy's mother.

"She was lonely, Willy. Real lonely, and I was, too, I reckon. We each of us got past the other's bad points and for a time it was good between us, Willy. It really was. She was upset you left like you did with no word or nothing. She needed comforting and that's what I tried to give her. It just all took off from there."

"But you left her high and dry in the end, Reese. In the end you cleaned her out and left her yourself."

"She sold the place 'cause of debts I incurred, because she loved me. I didn't clean her out, Willy. She cleaned herself out because she loved me. I only let her. It was wrong, I know, but I've always been of a certain desperate character. I ain't never tried to deny that. I tried to change, I really did. But a man can't change what he is, not even for love or nothing else when it comes down to it. A man always goes back to being what he was born to be. I can't help being what I was born to be, no more than you can help it, or no more than your ma could help it. We're all just what we are, Willy. Just what we are . . ."

Reese drank his way through two pots of coffee. Willy could see he was dying, could see the disease had eaten him up so far there wasn't nothing could be done for him.

"What about you, son?" Reese said. "Looks like you put some wear on you since I seen you last."

"I've gone down lots of trails too, Reese. I was a featured performer in Colonel Lily's Wild West Combination for a time. But I drifted off from that—on my own now, freelancing."

"I heard," Reese said. "I read about you in an advertisement in the newspapers once in Council Bluffs in a barbershop where I was getting my hair cut—before I became such a awful mess. I read all about you, Willy. I knew the first time I seen you shoot that little pistol of mine you were made for greater things than planting corn and butchering hogs."

"Yeah, well, like the Colonel told me when me and him parted ways: What I once was, I ain't no more."

"What's that supposed to mean?"

Willy reached into his shirt pocket and took out the

fold of down payment killing money, peeled off fifty dollars, set it by Reese's coffee cup, and said, "Take that, Reese."

"No, I couldn't take nothing more off you," he said without actually pushing the money back across the table.

"It ain't nothing, Reese. I got more where that come from. I ain't worried about it. Go on take it."

"Where you come by so much money, Willy? You ain't turned to a life of crime, have you, become some bank robber or something?"

"No, Reese. I ain't exactly yet."

Reese badgered him to know what he meant and Willy took out the wanted poster the man had given him to go along with the money and it had a likeness of the man he wanted Willy to kill—a man named Tristan Shade—and he set it on the table next and turned it around so Reese could see it.

"A man paid me to go find this fellow and kill him," Willy finally said. "You glad you know now? It make you feel any better you know, Reese?"

Reese swallowed like he had a lump of sugar in his mouth.

"You ought to reconsider," Reese said.

"Why's that?"

"Lots of reasons, but the main one is there is some things you end up doing you can't turn back from—like killing a man."

"Hell, Reese, don't worry. I'm sort of on the skids my ownself. Way I look at it, I don't have much more to lose than you."

Reese looked sorry then, looked off into the room toward the other diners, then toward the street beyond the oily window and hanging checkered curtains. It was like he was looking for something that no longer existed, but he wanted it to. It was a look of longing Willy saw in Reese's rheumy eyes.

"You was always a favorite of mine," Reese said softly.

"You was of mine, too," Willy said.

Then they didn't say anything for the longest time.

"Take that money, Reese, get yourself a room, a bed to sleep in, some food in you regular till you get things worked out."

Reese's eyes grew suddenly wet and spilled over.

"The good news is," he said, "I ain't got that long to work 'em out, Willy." Reese took the money and slipped it into his shirt pocket. "I can't promise you I can pay this back—you understand . . ."

"I ain't wanting you to pay it back. I'm giving it to you."

"Willy . . ."

"What?"

"Your ma . . . she died. I didn't want to have to tell you . . . But she died of something two years back. I went back to see her when I heard—her grave, I mean. I put some nice flowers on it—roses, which was her favorites—and told her I was sorry. But I knew it was way beyond her forgiving me . . ."

"Shit, Reese," Willy said, standing, adjusting the plainsman hat on his head. "You take care of yourself."

"Willy . . ." Reese said.

But Willy never looked back. Him and Reese were quits and he didn't want to know the outcome of things. He already knew enough to last him the rest of his life.

7

❧❧

"Now, where you think that peckerwood's really going?" Dallas said to Perk as they stood outside the bunkhouse, smoking.

"Get his tooth pulled?" Perk shrugged, he couldn't be sure the answer Dallas was after.

"Hell, we should have held him down and let you take your pliers and pull it out and see if it really was he had a bad tooth. I don't trust that boy. Anybody who'd drink with a nigger and whore with him."

"Sure," Perk said. "Whatever you say, Dallas."

Snow stood white over the grasslands and a man had to squint to look at it long. The horses nickered in the corral like they could smell freedom, their coats shaggy. Some of the boys were firing up the forge to shoe a few of the horses, and others were getting ready to go ride fence because the boss said it was easy enough to lose cows in this country and if it wasn't the cows busting down the fences on their own and getting lost, it was enterprising rustlers coming along with wire snips, cutting the fences and helping the cows get lost.

"It's been a lean year, boys," Bob Parker had told them. "Cain't afford no more losses or I might have to let some of you boys go." It worried them in a way, even though they told themselves they didn't care much for the work or the cheap wages. Still, a job was a job and hard to come by with winter setting in.

Taylor, Harvey, and Lon came over to where Dallas and Perk were leaning on the sun side of the bunkhouse, smoking, and Taylor said, "You gone ride with us to check them fences?" Mostly he directed his question to Perk and only obliquely to Dallas, who didn't do anything he didn't want to and they all knew you didn't tell him to do this or that.

Perk looked at him with those walleyes of his and shrugged and said, "I dunno."

"Listen," Dallas said to them. "We best keep an eye on that damn fool kid case he decides to say something that would set that law dog on us."

"Like what would he say?" Taylor said. "He don't know nothing. I mean he wasn't there with us when we . . ." Dallas cut him off with a sharp warning look.

"He don't have to know nothing. All he has to do is tell what he does know, about that nigger and the girl and me and you all."

Taylor stood there, his fists jammed down in the pockets of his mackinaw. His breath rushed out in smoky streams through his nostrils. Lon and Harvey stood without saying anything, mostly looking down, their noses red from the cold; Lon kept wiping at his with his coat sleeve.

"What you want to do about it?" Taylor said. "If he *is* saying something?"

"I don't guess we'd have much choice if he is, do you? I guess we'll have to put him under."

Taylor looked at Lon and Harvey, who didn't look up.

Their Stetsons were all sweat-stained and grimy from several seasons of dirt and dust, rain and fire smoke.

"Same goes for anybody else who wants to mix in with our business," Dallas added.

"That law dog, too?" Taylor said. "Is that what you're meaning?"

"That law dog, too, if we have to. Less of course you want to end up hanging down in Bismarck."

Taylor said, "We best go on and fix them fences for now." And with that he turned and Lon and Harvey fell in behind him as they headed for the corral to cut out saddle horses.

"You want I should go with them?" Perk said.

"No, you and me are going to ride into town and see what that kid is up to."

Perk sneezed and wiped his nose on his big red bandanna hanging around his neck and said, "Whatever suits you, Dallas."

"What girl?" Jake asked the kid.

"She lives just east of here. Her and a kid brother and their old mother. Some say she's a witch, the old woman is."

Jake said, "What's the girl got to do with any of this?"

"She was Dallas's gal before . . ."

"Before what?"

Tig rubbed his hands together and blew on them. *He is frightfully young*, Jake thought.

"Before Nat took up with her."

"She liked Nat better than Dallas? Is that it? Is that what happened, they got into it over a girl, Dallas and Nat?"

Tig nodded his head.

"That'd be my guess."

"But you don't know this for sure?"

"No sir. But I don't know no other reason they'd done what you say they did to old Nat. That's a pretty mean thing to do . . ."

"Yes, it is."

The youth's eyes brimmed with tears.

"I been trying to think on it, what it must have been like for him to be done that way. He was a good fellow, always happy. Pulled me out of a tight spot more than once. Nat was loyal to his friends."

"Were you his only friend, son?"

"I reckon on this outfit maybe I was."

"Tell me how I find this girl," Jake said.

The boy told him.

8

Johnny St. John was a bounty man and he'd been up in Bottineau County, hunting a man named Elmore Flogg wanted for train robbing, murder, and arson. Johnny caught him in an outhouse and Flogg shot Johnny's little finger off and it made him so damn mad that after Johnny killed him with three shots through the chest, he dragged him out of the privy and chopped his head off.

He built a little fire right there and cauterized the end joint of the shot-off finger by sticking his knife blade in the flames till it grew white hot and then seared it against the flesh.

He hopped around on one foot till the pain eased up, then kicked Flogg's head as far as he could kick it and watched it roll, then went and gathered it up and put it in a burlap sack, saying, "I'm gone take you back down to Bismarck and stick your fucken head in the window of the newspaper office so everyone can see you don't outwit or outrun Johnny St. John, you son of a whore bitch!"

Blood and some other things seeped through the bottom of the sack and the cold wind dried it to a hard rusty crust and if it had been hot at all the thing might have made Johnny's horse puke, but with it cold like it was, there wasn't much stink and Johnny thought sure it would still be in good enough shape to put in the newspaper's window down in Bismarck.

He'd ridden two days when he come across the stranger riding the same road opposite direction. They stopped there in the road for a brief moment, as was the custom among men in that country.

"How do," Johnny said. He was full of dope pills and whiskey because that was the way he lived—it was all that kept the demons in his mind at bay—the dope pills and whiskey was.

The stranger nodded and Johnny saw him eyeing the burlap sack tied to his saddle horn.

"I'm headed to Bismarck," Johnny said. "But I ain't et nothing but my own grub for two days now. There a town near here anywhere close a fellow could get some regular grub?"

The stranger thumbed back over his shoulder.

"Sweet Sorrow," the stranger said.

Jake had been on his way to see the girl—the one Tig told him about who was involved with Nat Pickett—when he saw the rider approaching along the north road. He was an odd-looking duck, wearing a tall beaver hat and a velvet coat. But it was the blood-crusted burlap bag hanging from the man's saddle horn that caught most of his attention.

The man asked him about a town, said he was headed for Bismarck. Jake told him about Sweet Sorrow.

"Appreciate it," the man said.

And then he looked down at the sack and said,

"Prairie chickens. I shot a bunch a while back and was planning on eating them for my supper, in case I dint come across no town."

"Well, then, I guess you saved yourself the trouble," Jake said.

The man said, "I reckon so."

Jake wanted to ask him what was really in the sack because it looked a lot fatter and heavier than prairie chickens. But he had no official cause to do so—and out here in this country, you just didn't get into a man's business without due cause.

But he opened his coat enough for the man to see the badge pinned to his sweater.

The man's eyes narrowed.

That son of a bitch is a lawman, Johnny told himself when he saw the badge. *And he wants me to know he is. Well, so the hell what if he is. I ain't done nothing illegal and if he asks, I'll show him the dodger on old Elmore here.* Somewhere it sounded like music playing in his head—music far off, like it was every time he took the dope pills and drank them down with whiskey overly much.

I could cut off your head as easily as slicing off a slab of beef, he thought, looking at the lawman's neck.

Jake waited for a second longer, then said, "I've got to get on. But know this, mister, I'm the town marshal back in Sweet Sorrow. I don't like trouble."

"Shit, you'll get none from me," Johnny St. John said. "Me and trouble is strangers."

"Yeah, that's what I would have guessed," Jake said sarcastically, for the man did not look like anything but trouble.

Jake touched heels to his horse and rode on, wondering at first if he might have made a mistake showing his back to the man in the red velvet coat and beaver hat.

Johnny St. John sat there staring after the lawman, thinking he had a pretty head.

"Me and trouble is strangers," he muttered, then laughed and anyone who would have talked to him for more than five minutes would know that Johnny St. John was crazy as a bedbug.

9

IT WAS A MILE, more or less, to the place. It looked like any other homestead upon the grasslands: simple and efficient. Jake was still getting the lay of the land, the people who had migrated to it, who they all were and where they had come from. As town marshal, he didn't have much reason to call on many of them who didn't live right in Sweet Sorrow. Unless, of course, there was a problem, some sort of trouble, like now.

The sun stood straight up and glaring off the snow. Warmer than you might think, the snow growing to slush in some places along the road. Jake loosened the buttons on his coat.

He dismounted in front of the cabin and knocked on the door.

"Are you Marybeth Joseph?" he asked when the door opened a crack and a face peered out.

"Who's asking?" the woman said. "If you're a drummer, keep moving. Got no need of anything and got no money."

Jake told her who he was, why he'd come: to speak to Marybeth Joseph. She looked him up and down.

"What's she done the law wants her?"

"Nothing," Jake said, "I'd just like to talk to her."

He heard another feminine voice say, "Oh, Mama, let the man come in, ain't you got no manners."

The door opened wide enough for him to enter.

There in front of the fireplace a boy sat in a copper tub, his hair soapy, and a young woman knelt next to him with a bar of scrubbing soap in her hand. Their eyes came to rest on the tall man. It was plain to see the young woman was heavily pregnant.

"Ma'am, my name is Jake Horn," he said, removing his Stetson and sweeping back the hair from his forehead. "Are you Marybeth Joseph?"

"I am," she said.

"You know why I want to talk to you?"

She shook her head. He guessed her to be hardly more than sixteen or seventeen; the older woman, maybe fifty; the boy, nine or ten. Marybeth Joseph was a big boney girl made bigger by her swollen belly. Broad face but cheerful eyes. Skin about the color of goat's milk and pitch-black hair twisted up into a bun atop her head and held with Spanish combs.

"No sir, I wouldn't have the slightest notion why you'd want to talk to me," she said. He could see, though, from the look she gave him that she *did* have some notion of what he wanted to talk about.

The old woman had gone and settled into a high-back rocker near the fire. There were several tintypes in tarnished frames atop the rough-hewn mantel. Stark, unsmiling faces staring out, and one of a young soldier holding a pistol in each hand across his chest. He had the look of a man about to be shot.

"Maybe we could have a private word," Jake suggested.

Marybeth Joseph stood with much effort and wiped

her wet hands on her skirts and said, "Let me get my coat." The old woman looked at her sharply, said, "What about Frisco?", moving her gaze to the boy in the tub.

"Maybe you could finish him up, mama."

The old woman said, "Lord . . ."

Once outside Marybeth Joseph said, "She had Frisco real late in life. Daddy was already dead by the time he was born. Died of consumption. Daddy would have been surprised he had it still in him to sire another one. Is eight years between Frisco and me. She likes to believe Frisco is mine and not hers; I'm like his ma to him." She rubbed her stomach with both hands on either side.

"How far along are you?" Jake said.

"Due anytime," she said. "I never had a little one. Sometimes it scares me."

"You know why I came, don't you, Marybeth?"

"Is it something to do with Nat?"

"It is," Jake said. "He is dead."

He saw her face crumple and she squeezed her eyes shut, as though trying to fight back whatever tears wanted to come. He thought she might lose her balance, but she steadied herself by leaning a hand against the door where the sun struck, turning the wood pleasantly warm.

"I'm sorry to be the one to have to tell you."

"They killed him, didn't they?"

"Who are *they?*"

"Dallas and them."

"You saw them take him out of here?"

"They wore masks, but I know it was them."

"Will you swear to that in a court of law?"

She looked uncertain then, turned her attention to the pigs rooting in a little wooden pen, tears coursing her cheeks.

The pigs rooted and snorted and pushed against one

another, trying to get at the slops. They reminded her of the way men were sometimes, rude and rough and mean. She looked at them with something akin to disgust.

"I can't get involved in all this," she said, her voice quaking.

"What was the trouble over?" Jake said.

"This," she said, patting her tummy. "It's what led to the trouble between them. Dallas might have thought this child I got in me is Nat's."

"Is it?"

She looked at him with her muddy brown eyes.

"I can't say, rightly. Could be Nat's, could be Dallas's. I guess I won't know until it comes out and shows itself."

"So Dallas suspected you and Nat were having relations."

"He accused me of it because someone told him they'd seen Nat's horse tied up out here. He slapped me around some next day and wanted me to tell him, but I was afraid he'd kill me, so I denied it."

"Do you know if Dallas ever threatened Nat?"

"Only to me, he did. Said he'd kill us both if he found out I was messing with him."

"I'll need you to testify against him," Jake said.

"Nat had a good soul, mister. You couldn't help but like him. He fixed our roof without me even asking and he took Frisco for horse rides and bought him candy, too. He was real nice to all of us."

"How come you didn't do anything when they took him?"

She shook her head.

"I don't know," she said. "I was scared. I figured they'd rough him up some, maybe run him off. Nat told me not to worry about it, said it was some sort of joke being played on him. I knew it wasn't no joke, but I was scared."

Tear spilled down her cheeks and she swiped them away with the edge of her hand.

"I can't risk it," she said. "He'll kill us all, me and Mama, and even Frisco was I to go against him. He'd kill this child, too." She rubbed her swollen belly, her eyes full of fear and remorse.

"You think he suffered much?" she said.

"No," Jake lied. "I don't think he did at all."

"That's good," she said.

A flock of geese went honking overhead, their calls starting out farther than the eye could see, then they appeared in a wavering V shape, their long dark necks extended, their wings drumming the air, their honk growing louder and louder, then fading away to nothing as though they'd never even existed.

"Will you go and arrest him?" she said. "Dallas, I mean?"

"I'm going to have a talk with him," Jake said. "Right now I've got nothing but suspicion to arrest him on. You're sure you didn't see their faces? I mean, even if you didn't and you knew for sure it was them, would you testify in a court of law to it?"

"I don't know," she said. "I mean, it could be Dallas's baby, too, I'm carrying. I don't know if I could say something against him to get him hanged, knowing it might be his . . ."

Jake started to turn to leave, then turned back.

"You got someone to help you deliver that child?" he said.

"Mama," she said.

He nodded and put a foot in the stirrup.

Marybeth Joseph said, "Wait," then went quickly into the house and returned again with a piece of paper in her hand. On it was written a name and an address: *Ophelia Pickett, General Delivery, Tulsa, OK Territory.*

"Nat give it to me just a few weeks ago, said if anything was to ever happen to him I should write his mother and let her know. But I don't reckon I could ever write such a sad letter to her. Least not now. I'd appreciate if you was to write her and tell her what happened. I'm sure she'd want to know."

Jake took the paper and put it in his shirt pocket.

He rode away, thinking *There are just some situations sadder than others, some folks who just don't stand a chance.*

10

❧❧

WILLY SILK THOUGHT, *If I'm gone kill a man, maybe I ought to practice. Thing is,* he wondered, *how do you practice killing a man without actually killing one?*

The train pulled into Bismarck, just as the sun settled onto the prairies like a bronze plate set on end, its last light spilling out over the grasslands.

Willy departed the train behind an old gent with a bent back using a cane to steady himself.

The old timer had told him during the ride that he had once been a fur trapper.

"Back in twenty," the old man said. "Got in near the end of it when all the beaver was about hunted out. Young buck like me didn't care. I wanted to go see the elephant, see what it was all about. Met Jim Bridger once at a rendezvous. Son of a buck could screw Indian gals like nobody I ever seen—have himself ten or twelve a night. Toss 'em out of his teepee when he was finished with 'em. They'd cry all over their daddies to let them marry him. But Jim wasn't the marrying kind, and when he had his fill of Indian gals and liquor and trading, why, off he'd go, by his lonesome. Didn't like partners no how. He said to me, 'You skinny little peckerwood, the Blackfeet is gone catch and scalp you, then stake you out to a termite hill after they cut yer pinions off.' I said to him, 'I ain't made of wood, I'm all flesh and bone, and they better bring a whole passel of 'em if they plan on cutting off my pinions' and he laughed like a son of a bitch and fell into a fire and had to be pulled out by his Indian gals."

Willy Silk had only half-listened to the old man. His mind was wanting to concentrate on how he was going to practice killing a human.

The old man said just before the train pulled into Bismarck, "Them cold creeks ruined me, wrecked my bones, give me the arthritis and the lumbago, bent my backbone like wire. Feels like I'm walking with stones in my shoes all the time. Gets worse ever year. I'll be so damn crooked of body when I die they'll have to bury me sitting up."

Then the train's whistle blew and the conductor announced "Bismarck" and the old man looked lost in his thinking and didn't say anything more. Willy waited impatiently for him to descend the step the conductor had put there.

"Take care yerself, young feller," the old man said over his shoulder as they walked away from the train, its belly shooting clouds of steam.

Willy stopped in at the first saloon he came to—the Union House. It wasn't the rowdy sort he was used to: stamped tin ceiling, long polished bar, pictures on the wall in gilt frames—one of Custer, one of Lincoln, both looking into the camera lens like they could read their future and saw it wasn't very good. The picture frames were still draped in black crepe. Imagine that.

Willy ordered a whiskey and a beer back.

"You ain't the new dentist, are you?" the barkeep said. "I got a rot tooth that's been nagging me like a wife for near a week now."

"I look like I make my living pulling teeth?"

The barkeep shrugged, said, "I'd not know what a man who makes his living pulling teeth looks like, but I'd buy him a bottle of the best whiskey in the house and help him drink it if he was to walk in here now."

"Hell no, I don't pull teeth," Willy said. Willy dropped back the flap of his coat enough to reveal the nickel-plated pistol he wore high on his hip. "That's what I do for a living," he said. "Case you was extra curious."

Willy drank in silence. The place was as dead as a funeral parlor.

"You got any whores working here?"

Willy'd figured out one thing all men enjoy was the company of a woman, and if you wanted to find a man who was of a desperate nature, such as the private detective Shaw had hired—Prince Puckett or the killer himself, this Shade fellow—then you might do best to get acquainted with the local whores. It was Bismarck where the money man said he'd last heard from Puckett.

The barman shook his head.

"We had a good one worked here once, but she quit and moved north. I heard she married a preacher and is out of the whoring business altogether. Then some fellow came through a few months back and hired four of old Sam Tolver's whores he kept over to the Bismarck Gentleman & Sports Club, the best whores this town ever had the privilege of knowing. So when it comes to whores, the town's a little low right now. Think the fel-

low who hired them was from some burg called Sweet
Sorrow, north of here, two days' ride. His last name was
Kansas. Odd name, Kansas, ain't it?"

"Jesus Christ, you always run off at the mouth so?"

The barman looked duly abashed and moved to the
other end of the bar, flipping his bar rag over his shoulder.

Time ticked away on the Regulator clock above the
back bar. The light grew dimmer until the barkeep went
around and lighted the hanging lamps that filled the
room with a soft buttery light.

Willy kept thinking about how he was going to practice his killing. Then an idea came to him and he called to
the barman: "Who's the worst no good son of a bitch
you know of around these parts?"

The man offered a sullen glance.

"Oh shit," Willy said, slapping an extra dollar on the
wood. "Don't mind me, I'm just in a bad mood from so
much traveling. Let me buy you a whiskey for that sore
tooth." This seemed to meet with the barman's ap-
proval.

"Apology accepted," he said and poured them each a
liquor. Willy noted how the barman kept the liquor in his
yap, allowing its medicinal properties to take effect on
his sore tooth and inflamed gums before gulping it down
like it was a whole egg.

"Well, now, let me see," the barman said, rolling his
eyes upward. "There's Blue Henderson, who can't get
along with nobody, lives out east of here a mile. Ever
time he comes to town he gets into a fight with somebody. Thinks men are always trying to flirt with his mis-
sus . . . real jealous type, but hard to see why, since Mrs.
Blue Henderson is ugly as a bucket of worms."

Willy Silk waited impatiently.

"Then there's Dobbs. Only he's the town marshal and is expected to be mean 'cause if he wasn't mean, nobody'd respect him. He likes to crack miscreants over the noodle with his pistol barrel. Says he learned the trick from some fellow named Wyatt Earp he used to deputy for in Dodge, Kansas . . ."

Willy poured himself another whiskey and refilled the bartender's glass as well . . . Jesus Christ, he was as slow a talker as Willy had ever encountered.

"But when it really comes down to the rub, I'd have to say the worst no good son of a bitch would be Champion Smith."

"Why's that?"

"He is rumored to have molested innocents, if you know what I mean."

"No, I don't know what you mean. Spell it out for me."

The barkeep leaned across the oak conspiratorially, putting his mouth near Willy's ear. Whether it was the liquor or the rot of the bad tooth, Willy could not ascertain, but the man's breath smelled rank.

"Screws animals and children, too, the way I hear it."

"How come this mean marshal of yours ain't locked him up, then?"

"Can't nothing be proved."

"Why not?"

"Well," the whiff of the barkeep's breath made Willy's knees go weak, but he withstood it because he thought maybe he'd found the one human he could practice killing on. "Animals can't talk and them kids won't. I think old Champion put the fear in 'em so deep and dark it stole their tongues."

"What's to say it ain't but rumor?"

"Nothing, I suppose. But two families has moved out because they thought old Champion was diddling their youngsters. And I am tempted to say the cows and goats and sheep and horses, too, run scared when they see old Champion coming down the street—but that would make light of a serious situation."

"Indeed, it would. Where might I find this Champion Smith?"

"Keeps him a dugout west of town—out a way from everybody else. He's a loner, never been married, stinks like a dung heap."

The mention of stink only added to the bad breath; it was all Willy could stand and he had to step away from the bar and out of smelling distance or he knew he'd pass out, then and there.

He stopped off at the general store and asked after cheap used pistols and purchased one had a pitted barrel and busted grips, but seemed to be in firing condition, then he rented a horse and rode out across the grasslands toward the west, keeping a keen eye for a dugout and didn't ride far before he spotted it. Rode up to the front of the place: Just logs stacked one atop the other with a tarp for a door and a mound of rusted cans off to one side. Staked out was a swayback dapple gray nag that looked wormy, its ribs and hipbones plainly showing through its sore infested hide. Willy wondered briefly if this Smith fellow had been diddling his own horse as well. It gave him the shudders to think what such a man was capable of.

"Hey, you ugly son of a bitch!" he shouted.

There was a lapse of time filled with naught but silence and a single plaintive cry of a lone meadowlark that balanced itself on a thick blade of brown grass, then fluttered off.

"Come on out here!" Willy yelled.

Finally the tarp of a door was drawn back and a scraggly-faced man in dirty clothes emerged.

"You Champion Smith?"

"Who the fuck's asking?"

"The man who has a proposition for you."

"A what?"

"Proposition, you damn fool."

"Go fuck yourself."

Willy drew his piece and aimed it at the man. He knew he could pop the dirty bastard's head and make it explode like a watermelon hit with a sledge. Only that would be too easy, wouldn't prove nothing. What he needed was to test himself against an armed man, somebody willing to shoot back. Only hopefully not somebody so good with a pistol the test might prove fatal.

"I'll shoot you where you stand," Willy said.

"Why the hell would you do that for?"

"Just for the hell of it, mostly. Now I want you to listen to my offer."

The man scratched his crotch.

"Pretty boy on a pretty horse," Champion Smith observed. "Hell, why don't you both come in and join me for a bit of repast?" His laughter sounded like wood breaking.

"Don't be a goddamn fool, old man."

"Make your offer, pretty boy."

"You any good with that pistol?"

"Good enough to shoot your dick off, though, that would be a shame . . ."

"I come to kill you, Champion Smith. And if you want to live you'll have to fight for the opportunity or die where you stand." Champion Smith went from scratching down below to scratching inside the nest of his head hair.

"Why you want to kill me, pretty boy? I never done nothing to you. Hell, I never even laid eyes on you till now."

"Because they tell me in town you're a no good son of a bitch who diddles cows and kids."

The man's nasty grin slowly disappeared.

"That so? That what they tell you? Well, don't believe ever goddamn thing you hear now."

Willy dismounted.

He reached into his pocket and took out the cheap pistol and tossed it in the dirt at Champion's feet.

The troubling thing was, the man showed no fear whatsoever. In fact, he seemed to enjoy the challenge Willy had laid down for him. Something cold ran down Willy's spine and he had to tell himself to remain steady, that it would be like shooting a glass ball or a game bird—only a lot bigger and thus a lot harder to miss. Willy holstered his own piece. The grungy fellow looked from the cheap pistol to Willy.

"Real pistol artist, eh?"

"You got about five seconds to reach for that iron," Willy said, "then I start pumping lead into you."

Champion Smith spat something that looked old.

"How I know that damn gun's even loaded?"

"Trust me, it is."

"Trust you, huh?" He bent slowly to pick it up, keeping his eyes on Willy the whole while. And when his hand touched it, he brought it up quick and Willy drew and fired and saw dust spank up from the man's shirt near his left shoulder and a small flower of blood bloomed through the ragged material. Champion Smith stepped back like he was trying to walk down a set of steps backward and missed one of them.

When he righted himself—momentarily examining the bullet wound through his shoulder meat—Willy could see the first bit of fear in the man's eyes.

"Your turn," Willy said. "Try again."

This time the codger didn't try and aim, just snapped off a shot from down near the hip where he was holding the gun. The shot probably killed the sky or the prairie, but it didn't come close to killing Willy. He was surprised at how calm he felt as he drew bead and shot the man again, this time through the ribs, even as Champion Smith quick fired two more shots.

Willy's bullet spun him around and he stood there for a moment, facing the wrong direction, like he was looking at the roof on his dugout for a leak and he was trying to figure out where exactly.

Then without rhyme or reason, Champion Smith fired the last two bullets into the side of the house. And when the hammer clicked, he turned around to face his foe.

"You want to reload?" Willy asked him.

Champion Smith seemed stunned speechless.

"Reload? What kinder damn idjit are you?"

Then the old man took notice of the blood leaking from his person, some of it spattering the toe of his boots, and he reached up with one hand and cupped it under some of the blood.

Willy reached inside his pocket again and took out a handful of shells and threw them at the man's feet.

"Go on, reload."

There was a pause, then Champion Smith said, "Hell, you gone shoot me either way . . ." as he squatted and picked up the bullets and replaced the spent ones in the chambers of the belly gun. He had a lot of trouble loading and dropped some of the shells and bent and picked them up again, his hands shaky, his fingers bloody and sticky. When he finally got all five in, he held the pistol with both hands and set to cocking it. And he got it raised and nearly aimed when Willy shot him a third time: just about where his belt buckle would have been if he'd been wearing a belt instead of a piece of rope tied to hold up his drawers.

It forced Champion to take a seat on the ground.

"It's like I got to go, only I can't," he moaned.

"I got to know something before I finish this," Willy said.

Champion Smith looked up at him, his eyes all anguish.

"Yeah, I did it," he said. "I diddled them kids and I diddled goats and horses and ever damn thing else come along. I've diddled women, too, but didn't like it nearly as well. I'm a diddling fool and I'd've diddled you, too, if I could have got my hands on you . . ."

"Diddle this," Willy said and shot him in the face—between moustache and bottom lip, the bullet breaking the man's teeth like a hammer.

Champion flopped back and did not move.

Willy stood contemplating the deed.

It wasn't at all what he figured it would be, killing another human. It left him with neither a sense of guilt, or of pleasure. *It was about like shooting a chicken for supper—something like that*, he told himself as he rode away.

Later that evening Willy located a whore at the Buffalo Head Saloon who said she had a previous encounter with one Prince Puckett: "Rough as a billy goat," she said.

And with further questioning, Willy learned Prince Puckett claimed to her he was indeed a man hunter and was after a particular fellow for a lot of cash money if he could find him and kill him and, she said, "Prince said he had a line on this particular fellow he was after, that he was north of Bismarck in some burg called Sweet Sorrow."

Willy thought, all in all, it had been a productive day.

That night Willy dreamed of his ma and him and Reese altogether in the farmhouse, him and his ma dancing while Reese played the fiddle. It shook him awake about the same time morning light crawled into the room.

Willy dressed and found a café where he ate a full breakfast and asked directions to the place the whore said, Sweet Sorrow, and was told that there was a stage line that ran up there if he wanted to take it.

Then he swung by the city marshal's office and said he had recently come past a dugout where a man lay outside shot dead and described Champion Smith to a tee and further said that not only was he dead as a coot but probably by now the fellow was being gnawed on by wolves and coyotes and that if the marshal wanted to find anything left to bury, he ought to get out there sooner rather than later.

The marshal was a stern-looking stout man with a broad flat face who said over his morning cup of coffee: "Well, at wouldn't be the worst news I heard this morning if the sucker you was talking about was Champion Smith. My only concern is that he will make them gnawing wolves and coyotes sick from eating him." Then he laughed at his own sense of strange humor and said, "Thanks for the information, mister. I might get round to it this afternoon or maybe tomorrow."

Willy went and waited for the stage. This man-killing business wasn't near as tough as he had thought it might be. He smiled and tipped his hat to a woman who walked past the train station. She did not smile back.

11

HE WAS SURE THAT DALLAS and a few of the other hands working Bob Parker's place had killed the boy, but he had no real proof. He wondered if he could legally arrest them on suspicion of murder. He just didn't know.

There at his desk he wrote the mother of Nat Pickett.

Dear Mrs. Pickett. The wet ink caught the light from the desktop lamp, then dried to a dull blackness . . . *I regret to inform you that your son, Nat, has passed away* . . . He tried to summon the right words, to make the news less ominous sounding, less tragic than it was. But how do you make the murder of a son sound less tragic?

He suffered an accident. I can assure you that all that could be done, was done. I've taken the liberty to see that he was interred . . . he thought about that word, then continued . . . *here in Sweet Sorrow, Dakota Territory, this day, Nov. 18th, 1881. If you have further questions regarding this matter, feel at liberty to write and I'll do my best to bring you whatever comfort I may. Most sincerely, Jake Horn, City Marshal*

He set the pen aside and stared at the letter. It seemed too little. He folded it and slipped it into an envelope and sealed it. Come morning, he'd walk it over the post office so that it would be sent on the next day's stage.

Clara came in, the evening sky just settling in to a dark rose. Her cheeks were red from the cold.

"Will you come to the house for supper?" she said.

"Do you think this is a good idea, Clara?"

"It's just supper, Jake. It's not a proposal for marriage."

He felt unable to tell her his mind, the fact that he couldn't really get involved with her, even though a large part of him wanted that.

"I think tonight's not a good idea," he said.

He saw the disappointment in her eyes, even though she did her best to hide it behind a forced smile.

"It's not a problem," she said. "I just thought you might like a warm meal someplace other than the café. Well, I really should get back to the girls. Take care of yourself, Jake."

He stood to try and explain, but she'd quickly turned and left. He went to the window and watched her go down the street, passing in and out of the lights of the businesses that were still open, until the shadows swallowed her.

He took his hat from the hook and slipped into his coat. The goddamn gun in his pocket felt like an intrusion, like something that should not be there. *What the hell you doing with this thing?* he asked himself, taking it out and looking at it. He set it on the desk, then went out. He was in need of a whiskey, something he could sip and let it do its work.

The Three Aces was in full swing. He ordered a whiskey, then found a table along one wall, directly below one of the new stuffed animal heads Ellis Kansas had ordered from a taxidermist in Bismarck. A pronghorn antelope that looked like it was still wondering what had happened to it stared with glass eyes.

There was laughter and good cheer in the room—or perhaps it was just the false bravado of men who drink too much. They talked loudly among themselves, trying to talk over the sound of the piano played by the skinny man in the top hat. Ellis's whores worked the crowd, their own particular laughter sharp and higher pitched, more forced than those of the men, enticing, falsely seductive.

Jake noticed the man he'd met along the road on his way to see the girl: The man in the dirty red velvet coat and beaver hat was standing at the bar. He was talking to a couple of others, the grimy burlap sack he'd had tied around his saddle horn now resting atop the oak. Ellis and his bartender were also talking to the man.

Then something strange.

Ellis poured the man a whiskey and the man untied the string from around the neck of the gunny and Ellis peeked in and drew back his head sharply as though punched.

The man in the velvet coat laughed. The others looked uncertain.

Jake could see Ellis pointing toward the door, saying something to the man in no uncertain terms. The man in the velvet coat stiffened, then tied the top of the sack again and pounded his fist atop the bar before taking the sack and stalking out.

Jake stood away from the table and went to the bar.

"What was that all about?" he said.

Ellis looked flushed.

"Son of a bitch had a head in that sack."

"Head?"

Ellis downed one of his own whiskies.

"Told him to take his fucken head and get out of my place! Warned him not to come back."

"He say what he was doing with it, how he came by it?"
Ellis shook his head.

"It was the head of a old Chinese, couldn't tell if it was man or woman."

Ellis looked like he was going to be sick.

Maybe a minute had passed since the confrontation, maybe two. But suddenly the man in the red velvet coat burst back in the front doors. This time he had a pistol in his hand and he came straight toward the bar.

"Oh, Jesus!" Ellis said.

"This is for you, mister," the man said and fired a shot that missed Ellis but shattered the back bar mirror.

Ellis ducked below the bar and came up with his own gun and returned fire, his bullet swiping the man's beaver hat off his head.

The whole population of the place broke into pandemonium.

The man fired again and so did Ellis, almost at the exact same moment. The man's second bullet caught Ellis in the neck and a stream of blood arced three feet into the air. Ellis dropped his piece there on the bar and grabbed his throat before falling like a broken vessel. The man in the velvet coat stood staring at the place where the saloon owner had been standing, thinking perhaps, he'd pop back up any minute. Folks were still trying to get out through the doors, front and back. Gunsmoke swirled in the oily light of the suspended lamps. The silence now that the shooting had stopped belied the sudden violence. Ears still rang.

The man said, "Well, I guess that son of a bitch won't ever mess with St. John again."

"That's your name, St. John?" Jake said. Every nerve fiber of his was taut, ready to snap. He cursed the fact he had left his own gun back at the jail.

The man looked at him, as though just now noticing there was someone else in the bar.

"That'd be me, mister, and if you want some of this, well, I'm ready to serve it up."

Jake raised his hands, said, "No, I don't want any."

The man's eyes worked over Jake like a birddog working a field, then narrowed and he said, "Say, you're the . . ."

Jake grabbed Ellis's pistol there on the bar.

Both men fired as one.

Jake's bullet tumbled the man off his feet. He went down kicking, holding his chest, making strange noises.

The man said, "God*damn*, god*damn* . . ."

Jake knelt next to him and yanked the pistol from his hand. He didn't want to let it go, but did.

"That was a stupid thing you did," Jake said. "Stupid and senseless."

"Yeah . . . maybe . . ."

Then the man took one large gulp of air and stopped breathing.

Jake went around back of the bar. Ellis was lying there in a pool of bright red blood, the wound in his neck pumping less now, down to just a squirt. Ellis's face was blanched, his eyes all whites. Jake took a bar rag and pressed it to the wound. Ellis's eyes rotated until their dark centers showed again. He tried to talk, but a bloody foam bubbled out of his mouth instead of words.

Several of the previous customers had drifted back in, now that the shooting had stopped, some having the bravado to, once safely outside, peek through the windows. Jake enlisted several of them to carry Ellis over to Clara's—Doc Willis's old place and the infirmary he kept there.

Clara answered the knock and saw the men carrying

Ellis and led them back to the infirmary, where they laid Ellis on a exam table. Jake set to work, saw that the bullet had passed between windpipe and vertebrae, thus saving Ellis from certain death or paralysis. He had one of the men go and get snow in a pan and bring it in and began packing it around the wound. He did this over and over again until the bleeding clotted, then took needle and thread and stitched closed the blood holes, entry and exit, and wrapped Ellis's neck tightly as possible with a bandage.

The men who'd helped carry Ellis over couldn't hardly stand to watch such doings as a man's bloody flesh getting sewn like a piece of ragged cloth and had drifted off back to the saloon and continued their drinking. They had something more worthwhile to talk about than the weather or complain about their wives or low wages or no work at all. A good gunfight was good for business. It made men thirsty and randy, too, it seemed. It got them stirred up thinking about how quick things can be over, how temporary life is, and by god if there was anything they'd thought about doing but hadn't yet, they ought to quick get to it or they might not ever get the chance. Ellis's girls were still shaken by the sudden turn of events and they weren't in much of a mood to practice their trade considering, but they were practical-minded women, too. It could be Ellis would die and the place would close and they'd be out of work tomorrow or the day after tomorrow and none of them had saved much money because it wasn't their way to, even though that was about all they ever talked about: how they were going to save their money and get out of the trade.

So they did what they knew how to do and the drinking and fornicating went on that night as usual, even if Ellis getting shot was in the back of their minds.

Ellis fell in and out of consciousness. Jake finally managed to get a spoonful of laudanum down him for the pain, then went out into the other room, where Clara sat at the kitchen table alone.

"Girls in bed?" Jake said.

She nodded.

"Men," she said.

"Yeah," he said. "I'm sorry to bring this to your door."

He poured himself a cup of coffee. Noticed that his cuffs were bloodstained, tried to hide them, but he saw her staring.

"You're a doctor, aren't you?" she said.

"Yes," he said.

"Then why hide it?"

"Do you really want to know, Clara?"

"Yes," she said, "if you're ready to tell me."

"Okay then, I'll tell you."

And when he'd finished telling her about the night he had been falsely accused of murder by the woman he loved, the whole shameful incident of betrayal and infidelity, he sat back and waited for her reaction.

"You made a mistake, an error in judgment," is all she said. "It could happen to anyone."

"I think I deserved what I got," he said. "I cuckolded another man, I broke my Hippocratic oath, I was immoral as well as stupid."

"Yes," she said. "You made a mistake. You fell into a trap because you loved the wrong woman. Which of us hasn't made bad choices in giving our hearts to the wrong one? It doesn't mean you aren't a good person, that you don't deserve some peace and happiness."

"It doesn't change the fact that a man was killed," he said. "There's nothing I can do to prove my innocence.

That's the really damn frustrating thing. It's my word against hers. And someday, the law or a bounty hunter will come looking for me and I'll have to either run or fight. And if whoever it is doesn't get me the next time, they will the time after. Sooner or later, I'll pay the ultimate price. Now you know why I can't let myself get involved with you, Clara. I can't put you in that danger."

She closed her eyes for a long moment, then opened them and looked directly at him.

"I know a little about betrayal," she said. "I know what it is to be fearful that someone who wants to harm you will come looking for you. You're right, about putting me in danger. But if it were just me, I wouldn't care. But I have the girls. I can't let them be put into danger . . ."

Into the night he went again, the air chill, the feeling still lonesome. Jake walked back to his hotel. He felt exhausted, emotionally drained. He lay upon the bed, thinking about the events of earlier. Someone knocked on his door and he answered it. Gus Boone stood there with the burlap bag.

"Go bury that damn thing," Jake said.

"He left it on the sidewalk outside of the Three Aces."

"Go bury it."

Gus looked forlorn.

Jake reached into his pockets and found a dollar.

"Here. Go bury it."

"Yes sir."

Jake closed the door. He wished it would close out everything. That the world would forever remain outside his door.

*   *   *

Outside Gus felt snowflakes falling on his eyelashes, said to the head in the sack, "Sorry about all this, mister, or ma'am, or whatever you are . . ."

It was otherwise a pretty night.

12

❧❧

THEY WERE WAITING FOR HIM when he returned from town. Dallas and Perk and the others.

"How's that tooth?" Dallas said.

Tig started to say, "What tooth?", then remembered the excuse he'd given for going in to see the city marshal.

"Doc lanced it, said it didn't need to come out. Two glasses of whiskey and it's all but healed. Guess I'm the lucky one, huh."

Sun glared off the snow, making it look like shattered glass. The horses moved about in the corral, their coats grown shaggy.

"You do anything else while you was in town besides get that tooth looked after and drink a couple of whiskies?"

Tig dismounted and began undoing the cinch strap, keeping his back to the others.

"No," he said over his shoulder. "Like what?"

"I dunno, go have a talk with that lawman, for instance?"

"No, I didn't."

Tig pulled his saddle and blanket off the horse, then walked it over to the corral and turned him out with the others, slapping the palm of his hand on the muscled flank, saying, "Git on in there."

Perk was smoking a cigarette and staring with those crazy eyes of his when Tig turned around. The others were watching him careful, too. Dallas especially.

"You know nobody wants trouble round here because of that colored," Dallas said.

"That includes me," Tig said, feeling once more disloyal to his dead friend. But what could he do about it. Wasn't nothing he could do, was there? He'd done what he could by talking to the lawman. Nat couldn't expect nothing more of him.

They closed in on him, slowly like they might a critter they were hunting. He raised his hands, said, "Whoa up, boys. What's going on here?"

"I been thinking," Dallas said.

"About what?"

"About that tooth of yours."

"I told you, the doc in town took care of it."

"Maybe so, but I know that dentist is the biggest damn drunk in the whole of Dakota and was I you I wouldn't trust him. Why, I once knew a feller in New Mexico who died of a bad tooth—real bad death, too. Suffered terribly. Said it put poison in his blood and it ended up killing him. I'd sure enough hate to see such a thing happen to you, being as good a hand as you are."

Perk said, "Yah, we sure would hate to see something like that happen to you, kid."

Then someone tossed a lariat over him from behind and yanked it tight and he saw it was Taylor and when he tried to yell, Perk come up and stuffed a dirty bandanna into his mouth and said, "Shut up, goddamn you!"

Wasn't no way he could fight them off. He thought of Nat, how they probably had done the same thing to him, grabbed and carried down to the creek, the fear filling him up like water into a bucket.

His eyes bugged toward the main house, hoping the boss would come out to see what the commotion was and stop things before they got too far out of hand. But the house stood silent, and as Tig's gaze swept the house, he could see the brougham that the boss used to travel in was not parked where it usually was. Him and his wife gone, nobody to help him.

His boots scraped along the ground as they half-dragged, half-carried him to the bunkhouse. And when they slammed the door shut behind them, its bang sounded like a gunshot and he could almost feel a bullet piercing his heart.

"Hold him down good, boys!" Dallas said. "Perk, go get them pliers."

He struggled until Dallas slammed his fist into the side of his face, a blow that stunned him and caused his ears to ring.

"There's a little medicine to help ease the pain coming," Dallas said.

Tig could feel the end of his nose stinging and the warm flow of blood coming from it.

Somebody, Taylor maybe, pulled the bandanna out of his mouth and he took a great gulp of air before a wooden spoon was inserted. He bit down, but they pried his jaws apart. Then he saw those floating unsettled eyes of Perk looking down at him, his face so close he could smell Perk's whiskey breath warm and thick.

"I got my plars," Perk said and showed him the tool. "Which tooth you say it was again?"

Tig closed his eyes, his strength all but gone out of him now. The hands that gripped him—one had put a knee into his chest with his whole weight behind it—were too strong. Tears leaked from his eyes as he felt the invasion of the pliers, the taste of that hard metal against his tongue.

"Shit," Dallas said, "might just as well pull two or three of them to make sure we got the right one."

"And I only charge a dollar a tooth," Perk said with a snigger.

Tig felt the pliers clamp down on his front tooth, felt the pinch of them against his gums, felt the unbelievable force applied, followed by a lightning of pain. It felt as though his head was exploding, as though he was going to bite off his own tongue as Perk levered the tooth. He screamed. A twist and a yank and the tooth tore out. Perk held it close to the lamp one of them held, its root bloody, the rest white as a piece of porcelain.

"There's one," Perk said, breathing hard. "Let's get the otherns."

Later Tig lay alone in the darkness, the bunkhouse empty—he'd heard them getting ready to go into town, talking about drinking and gambling and whoring. Laughing and jesting with each other, as though what they'd done to him meant nothing to them.

His whole face throbbed, his mouth so swollen he could barely swallow.

Dallas had stopped by the bunk on his way out and said in a low menacing voice: "I'm sure you're gone thank me when you get around to feeling better. 'Cause what we did for you was save your life, you see. Hell, tell you what, kid, you can buy us a drink next time we're in town together. Oh, and don't worry about them three dollars Perk said he was going to charge you for the teeth pulling. It wouldn't be right, him not being a real dentist. You just remember something, boy, there are some things nearly bad as dying. And if I hear anything about you running your mouth to that lawman about me and that nigger, well, you'll end up like him."

Tig tried to lift himself out of bed to get a sip of water, but the pain was too great and he fell back dizzy. And in that moment he hated Nat.

If you hadn't gone and messed with that girl . . .

He raised a hand and lightly touched his face—it felt strange and painful, even to the slightest brush of his fingertips. Felt all misshapen.

He unknotted the bandanna from around his neck and with great effort and fighting down the bloody torment it took to do it, he tied the bandanna around his head and jaw, then sat up slowly, steadying himself to keep from falling back again. It took a long time, it seemed, but he finally got a few belongings stuffed into his saddle bags: extra shirt, pair of socks, razor, Barlow knife, the tintype of his sweetheart, Hester, back in Nacadocious, Texas. Then he went out into the steely cold night and saddled his horse, nearly feinting twice in the doing. He could see lights on in the main house now, the brougham parked where it usually was. Tig had a week's pay coming, but he didn't know if he had the heart or nerve to go up to the house and ask for it. He felt duly embarrassed by his condition. But without that week's pay, he was flat broke.

It was hard to present himself in his condition, but hell, he had no choice.

He knocked and in a moment the door swung open and Bob Parker stood there staring at him.

"What the hell happened to you?"

He tried to say, but only mumbled, "I . . . come . . . for . . . my . . . p . . . pay."

"What? I can't hardly understand what you're saying."

He repeated it, each word feeling as though he was taking a bullet to the face.

Bob Parker shook his head and said, "Wait a minute," and closed the door again. The air felt like cold iron pressed to his bare skin and caused his pain to increase. He wanted to scream, but instead stood there shaking.

The door opened again and Bob Parker handed him a week's pay.

"I was probably going to have to let some of you boys go, anyway," Bob Parker said. "I guess this works out okay. You fall off your damn horse or something?"

Without further effort to explain anything, Tig turned and put a foot in the stirrup of his saddle and pulled himself up onto his horse, tapped his heels, and didn't look back at the house as it receded into the night.

The whole of the sky was shotgunned with stars and he'd never been so miserable. He didn't know where he would go or what he'd do once he got there. He just knew that if he stayed, he'd most likely end up like Nat, murdered in a horrible way. The road north led to uncertain places. All he knew that lay north was the Canadian border, eventually. He turned the horse south. If he could make it as far as Bismarck, he could sell his horse and saddle for a ticket to get him maybe down to Texas. He'd like to see his sweetheart again. It had been almost two years since he had been with her. He recalled her last words to him there under a broiling sun.

"Dakota?" she'd said. "Whatever is there for you in Dakota?"

"I hear a man can easy put together a small spread, that the country is full of stray cows and wild horses. They say the grass is high as your head, so it's a lot of free graze."

He remembered the soft denim blue of her eyes, the

sprinkle of cinnamon freckles across her pert nose. He remembered, too, the soft warm parts of her body. Tears flowed down his face.

Nacogdoches, he thought. *If I can just make Nacog-doches.*

But he'd have to get past Sweet Sorrow and Dallas and them who were there now, drinking and laughing and whoring. He'd have to avoid letting them catch him. And yet if there was anything he needed worse than a bottle of whiskey to see him through this night, he couldn't imagine what it was. His mouth hurt like it had been hammered and every step his horse took was like getting hammered all over again.

He'd need something to kill the pain and whiskey was the only something he knew and Sweet Sorrow was the only place he knew to get it.

He saw a star shoot across the heavens.

Nat, he thought. *Is that you, Nat?*

13

❖❖

DALLAS AND PERK AND THE OTHERS were drinking in the Three Aces. Customers were still talking about the shooting earlier. Even though the bartender, Handsome Harry, had mopped up the blood, the stains of the gun battle's victims still showed dark in the flooring.

The drinkers leaned on their elbows as they listened to Gus Boone tell how a man who had him a head in a sack came in and shot Ellis Kansas and how the marshal in turn shot the man with the head.

Dallas said, "Real gun artist your marshal, is he?"

Gus Boone nodded and said, "I seen ever bit of it, was standing right here, almost took a bullet myself. Marshal Horn was a real cool customer. Shot that feller like he was a rat going after the cheese."

The others looked to their leader, Dallas. He knew they were waiting for him to say or do something, they didn't know what—just something.

What he said was "Let's get us up a poker game."

The smoke, the sweat of flesh, the noise, all seemed to press together in that long narrow bar. New arrivals came in, slapping their hands together and shaking a fresh-fallen snow from their hat brims.

"God*damn* but it's cold and getting colder," they said, moving first to the woodstove before going to the bar.

But the whiskey and the prospect of bedding one of the whores, who kept a steady trade headed to the back rooms, soon warmed their blood and they took up chairs of those leaving to go home to their wives, or their bunkhouses or rented rooms.

And the story of the shooting continued to circulate, changing a bit each time, getting off center from the facts until each man who heard it had his own version to tell later on, a year from now, or maybe someday to their grandkids.

Across town Ellis Kansas moaned from the throat-clutching pain in his neck. Clara left a book she was reading to look in on him. She could almost feel the fever coming off him, wet a cloth and put it on his forehead.

"Shhh, Mr. Kansas," she said softly. She held the lamp up close to the bandage around his neck. It caused her to cringe slightly when he turned his wide-eyed gaze to her, his flesh an odd dark color now, like rotted plums, as though the stanched blood was pooling in his face.

"*Mmmmph . . . Mmmmph . . .*" he mumbled.

"I can't understand you, Mr. Kansas," she said. "Please try not to talk. I don't think it's good for you."

His hand came up and his fingers felt of the bandage and it caused him to close his eyes. "*Mmmmph . . .*"

"Do you want me to get the . . ." She had started to say "doctor." "Do you want me to get someone to help you?"

He wagged his head no.

She uncorked the bottle of laudanum and put it to his mouth. Like a child, his lips nibbled at the bottle until he had gotten some down. She saw the scrunch of his features as he swallowed.

"Try and rest, please," she said.

She waited until his face slackened, then went out of the room again.

The hour late, the girls abed, she thought about Jake Horn and her desire for him. The grasslands—indeed the whole of the West—was such a lonely place for a woman. She went out onto the porch and took in a deep breath of cold air and the snow swirled around her and it felt good in a way to feel it on her face. Even though she was beginning to be sure how she felt about him, Jake had given her no reason to hope and it felt like disappointment to her. *Is this what I want?* she asked herself. *To be in love with a man who doesn't seem to have a future?*

The pain in Tig's mouth was a fire. By the time he'd reached the outskirts of Sweet Sorrow, his tears had frozen in his thin moustache. The brim of his hat carried half an inch of snow and his fingers were numb. He could barely stand to breathe.

He saw the light of the saloon. It seemed to him a beacon of salvation, even though he realized the risk he was taking—had to take—in order to find some measure of relief. Twice he'd stopped along the way and tried to eat snow. It was like eating cactus needles.

He considered for a long painful moment skirting the town and going on, but knew that it was nearly impossible to go any farther without some sort of relief for his pain. All the relief he could hope for was in that saloon.

He touched his heels to the belly of the horse and rode toward that single beacon of light.

I'd as soon be dead as to go on like this, he told himself. The will and resolve he had in him until that point shattered like ice hit with a hammer and he rode toward the town no longer caring what happened to him if he could just find a little relief.

How long Jake had been sleeping when he was awakened by a pounding on his door he couldn't say. It seemed like he'd just closed his eyes.

"Marshal!"

He crawled out of bed and answered the door.

Gus Boone stood there with the stink of liquor coming off him.

"You better come'n, there's 'bout to be another shooting over to the saloon."

"Christ . . ." he muttered, pulling on his trousers and boots. He tucked in his nightshirt and pulled on his coat and went down the stairs hatless, following Gus out across the street through the fresh snow.

"What's going on over there, Gus?"

"Them Double Bar boys are about to get into it—one of them is, anyway."

Jake remembered then he'd left his gun at the office.

"You heeled?" he said to Gus.

"No sir, I am ashamed to admit it, but I traded my old gun for a jug some time ago and ain't been able to afford another since."

Wind swirled snow in the street. The lights of the saloon peeked out from the front windows. There was no piano music. Bad sign.

Jake stepped in through the doors, Gus right behind him.

What was going on was going on toward the back of

the place. The gathered parted a path when they saw Jake.

The boy, Tig, stood at the end of the bar facing Dallas and the others with him who'd fanned out around a poker table. Dallas wore his revolver in a cross-draw holster and the others were similarly heeled as well.

The tension between the two was heavy; the only thing moving was the swirl of cigar smoke in the oily light of the hanging lamps.

"Go on, boy, go for your piece and let's settle this," Dallas was saying when Jake came into the fray.

Without hesitation Jake stepped in front of Tig and said, "What the hell's going on?"

The boy's face was a mess.

Tig's eyes flickered with pain and anger as he refused to look directly at Jake but stared beyond him toward Dallas and the others.

Tig started to raise a hand to point at Dallas, but Jake slapped it away and jerked the revolver from the boy's holster, then turned on Dallas and said, "You do that to him?"

The puncher's eyes narrowed.

"This ain't none of your business unless you want it to be."

"See, here's the thing," Jake said, thumbing back the hammer of the single-action Colt. "No matter how fast you think you are"—Jake brought the pistol straight out—"you're not going to be fast enough. I've already killed one man here tonight and I guess I must be getting used to it, because I'm more goddamn mad about being woken from my sleep than I am about the possibility of murder right now. So it's your choice: You can either clear the hell out of here or show these boys what a gunfighter you are."

Jake understood if he showed Dallas Perk the least bit of hesitation or fear, the man would kill him.

He could see the probabilities running through that thick head of the puncher, wondering if he could pull his gun and get off a good shot before Jake pulled the trigger on him or if he couldn't.

Dallas silently cursed himself for drinking too heavily and not thinking clearly and shooting that damn kid when he first came in. Thinking the kid must have been crazy to walk in like he did, knowing they'd be there. That snot nosed little son of a bitch was a mama's boy and they should have put him under when they had the chance. Now this interfering lawman had put himself into it, had gotten the drop on him.

"I could tell these boys of mine to shoot you out of your boots," Dallas threatened.

"But you won't because you know that won't stop this first bullet."

Another moment of hesitation, then: "Okay," Dallas said. "We'll leave. Come on boys."

The others didn't move for a moment until Dallas looked at them hard and said it again.

"Leave the guns," Jake said. "Put them on the table."

"You got no right!"

"My town, my rules. Put them on the table. You can send one of your men in tomorrow to pick them up."

"Fuck that!"

"I'm not going to stand here all night. Do what I said or fight, goddamn you!"

Jake knew he'd already cowed the man or Dallas would have pulled his gun by now. A man with bad intentions didn't stand around talking.

"I'm already on edge, so do it slow," Jake said when

Dallas moved his fingers toward the pistol. Once deposited, Jake waved him off and waited for the others to follow suit until all five had put their pistols on the table.

Jake followed them out the doors and waited until they mounted their horses.

"Stay out of my town," he said.

"You pushed things too far," Dallas said with a growl. "We're going to come back and we're going to settle matters once and for all. Ain't no smooth-hand son of a bitch going to tell me where I can and can't go. You want a fight, well, by god, you just bought yourself one. Get ready, mister, because hell's going to come down on you like a hard rain."

Jake stood sucking in the cold air until the sound of hooves faded into the crimson night, then returned to the bar.

Tig stood sipping whiskey through his ruined mouth.

Jake slipped the revolver back in the kid's holster and said, "You want to tell me what's going on?"

Then the boy drew back his upper lip, his face lined with pain, and showed the bloody gums where the teeth had been yanked out.

"They do that to you?"

Tig nodded.

"Why?"

The boy shook his head.

He flinched every time he took a sip of whiskey.

"Come on, I've got something better than that for you," Jake said.

Jake waited until the laudanum caused the boy to close his eyes, then dropped the key to the room he'd rented for the kid there on the nightstand next to the bed before going down the hall to his own room.

Jesus! he thought. *What the hell sort of men are these who would murder Nat Pickett and now disfigure Tig?* But he already knew what sort of men they were. And he knew that they'd be back, and the next time it would be a war when they came and he'd better be ready.

14

❧

MORNING SUN FILLED THE WINDOW and fell into the room where he slept.

He dreamt of a drowning boy, and one with the busted mouth of a jack-o'-lantern. He dreamt of women and horses and war. And when at last he stopped dreaming and came out of his fitful sleep, he swung his feet over the side of the bed and sat there for a painful moment, trying to bring some warmth into him. The small wood stove in the room had grown cold and there was frost on the inside of the windows. He ran his fingers through his hair, then dressed, the cold leather of his boots stiff around his feet.

He went to the basin and dipped his fingers into the pan of cold water, lifting it over his face, the droplets clinging to his beard, then rubbed dry with the small fresh towel, donned his hat and coat, and went down the hall to where Tig's room was and knocked on the door.

The boy answered after several moments, his face puffy and misshapen. The bruising around his mouth was especially disturbing to see. The boy didn't try and speak this time but turned aside and went back and lay on the bed, turning his face to the wall as though ashamed to have anyone look at him.

Jake reached inside his coat and took out a pencil and a sheet of paper and said, "I want you to write it down."

The boy didn't respond.

"I want you to write it down what they did to you. I want your written testimony, then I'll arrest them."

The boy turned over slowly and looked at him. Jake handed him the pencil and paper.

"You know how to write?"

The boy nodded and wrote something on the paper, then handed it back to Jake.

They wont to kil me.

"Because they know you know that they murdered Nat . . ."

The boy shook his head and pointed at Jake.

"Because they know you came and talked to me?"

Tig nodded.

"Will you testify in a court?"

Tig shook his head again. No.

"Then they'll get away with it."

The boy wrote again, taking the paper completely out of Jake's hand and holding it against the wall.

I dont ker.

Jake took the paper, folded it, and put it in an inside pocket.

The boy sat forlorn, his forearms resting on his knees, the dirty lank hair hanging in his eyes.

Jake pointed to the bottle of laudanum, said, "Take a swallow of that when the pain gets too bad to stand, then when you feel up to it, go see the dentist, see if he can stitch up your mouth. Perhaps he can make you some porcelain teeth."

Tig nodded. Jake turned to leave, then paused at the door, turned, and said, "Sometimes a man's got to fight for himself or he might just as well be dead. I could go into a long sermon on how sometimes a man has to fight for his friends as well, how if the shoe was on the other foot and it had been you they murdered and Nat that had lived, you'd hope he'd do something to bring your killers to bay. I could talk all damn day about friendship and morality and what's right and wrong, but I'm not going to. You do what you have to, son. Fight, or leave, or just sit here in this room. Your choice."

Jake called upon the men who more or less made up the town council, the ones who paid his wages—business owners: Otis Dollar, the merchant; Cheerless Carl, the barber; Tall John, the undertaker; Marcus Fold, the dentist; and Ted Lawton, the attorney and realtor who owned most of the town lots; and Ernst Hollingshead, the banker. The only one not there was Ellis Kansas. Jake reminded himself to check on the saloon owner soon as the meeting was finished.

They met in Hollingshead's office at the back of the bank.

"I've got a problem," Jake began, then proceeded to tell them about the trouble with Dallas Fry and the rest of the Double Bar boys.

"I think they'll come to kill me because they know I'm going to arrest them for the murder of that Negro cowboy, Nat Pickett."

Lawton was the first to speak to the matter, accustomed as he was to serious situations.

"Then perhaps its best you resign and find somewhere else to reside, Mr. Horn," he said.

Jake looked at him hard.

"That's your answer? What then, if I quit and leave?

You going to take up the badge and handle the problems here? And if you do, and Dallas Fry decides he wants to kill or run you off too, are *you* going to tuck tail?"

"I'm just saying that sometimes avoidance of a problem is the best solution. At least it seems so in this instance. What do you propose the rest of us do about it?"

"Trust me. What you're suggesting is not the best solution."

The banker, Hollingshead, said, "Are you asking us to take up guns and fight with those boys?"

"I think we all need to be together on this," Jake said. "I need you to stand with me when they come. If they see a show of force opposing them they might just give up the guilty parties and let justice have its day."

Marcus Fold said, "Hell, I'm just a dentist. I don't know anything about gunfighting!"

"Neither do I," Carl said. "I'd be useless in a gunfight . . . I'd probably be the first one killed."

Jake looked at the others, their eyes lowered, except finally John said, "If you need me to do it, I will, but I don't like the idea much. I'm no gunfighter, either. None of us are."

"Otis?" Jake said.

But Otis Dollar simply shook his head while staring at the toes of his shoes. He had not forgotten how Jake had rescued his wife a couple of months earlier when she'd been kidnapped by the mad Swede. And he prayed silently that the marshal wouldn't throw it up in his face now and force him to admit to his own cowardice.

"Lawton?" Jake said, instead.

"I've no heart for bloodshed either, Mr. Horn. I wish I could say that I did, but my business depends on me remaining neutral in this matter. No, I'm afraid you shouldn't count on me."

Jake had to tamp down his anger. This wasn't their fight; it was his and he was asking them to put their lives at risk for him in a fight they knew they couldn't win. Whatever he'd done for this town and the people in it was yesterday's news. It was what they paid him to do.

Of the bunch only Tall John was willing to stand with him, even if reluctantly so. But he knew that to coerce a man to go against his instincts could be a fatal mistake.

There was only one other man Jake could think of who might pitch into the fight with competence and grit: Toussaint Trueblood. Toussaint had backed him before in a fight.

He turned and went down the stairs and could practically feel their stares on his back.

The old woman—the pregnant girl's mother—was there in front of the jail, sitting atop her wagon, bundled in an old coat with a heavy wool scarf tied around her head. She looked up when he approached.

"It's time," she said. "Marybeth's water's broke, but that babe's in her wrong. I need someone to help me."

Jake climbed up onto the wagon and took the reins.

"How did you know I could help?" Jake asked.

"She said she knowed you'd help, that she had a dream about how you come in the night to her, that you reached inside her body and took out the babe . . ."

Jake put the horse into a quick trot, thinking, *Everything about the girl and Nat seems star-crossed, like the only luck to be had is just the bad.*

Jake could hear the girl's moans before he reached the door, wails really. The boy, Frisco, sat on a chair staring dumbly at the girl. Her eyes came around, wide and white, when Jake approached her bed.

"Take it out of me," she said.

"It's not that simple," he said. He turned to the old woman and said, "I'll need hot water." Then, turning back to the girl, he said, "Marybeth, I'm going to put my hands on you, I'm going to feel the position of the child." She nodded.

"Steady your breathing," he said and she stopped her chuffing while he ran his hands over her hard smooth belly. The old woman had been right: The child was turned the wrong direction.

Jake took the extra pillows on the bed and propped them under the girl's hips.

"I'm going to start pushing down," he said. "I'm going to try and get the baby to turn."

"Don't let it die . . ." she said. "Don't let *me* die . . ."

"I won't."

But he knew that there was every chance one or both of them *would* die if he couldn't get the child turned. He began to gently but forcibly push down with his hands at one end of the lump. Sometimes such maneuvering worked in breech births, but the odds were against it. The girl moaned. Jake released the pressure momentarily, then began to push again. Twice over the next hour something under the skin fluttered, a knee, a foot, a hand, but still the infant refused to turn.

He could see the girl was losing strength. Her color was nearly as pale as the bed sheets. He felt himself losing the battle. Over and over again he tried manipulating the babe into position—head down into the birth canal. But there was no movement over the next half hour and he suspected maybe the child was stillborn. If it was, the girl's only chance was for him to open her up and take it in an attempt to save her life.

He leaned in close and touched her face with a dry towel and wiped away the droplets of sweat.

"Marybeth . . ." he said. She looked up at him. He could see the fear, the knowing fear that a woman would sense when everything had gone wrong.

"I may have to take the child," he said. "Do you understand what that means?"

She moved her head back and forth just barely, her eyes full of deep questions.

"It might be too late to save the baby, but I can try and save you."

"No!" she cried.

He felt helpless, even as he placed his hands against her belly one more time. This time his fingers trying to surround the tiny head, hoping to somehow transfer his need for it to turn in order to save the girl—the very life of its mother. He worked his hands in the way he'd been taught in medical school, summoning every fiber of his will if not his strength to get the baby to turn, pressing and moving, manipulating. It resisted. He knew he must make a decision quickly and said to the old woman, "I'll need a sharp knife. Clean, let it set in the boiling water, then bring it to me. I'll need needle and thread, too, lots of thread."

Then suddenly the baby turned as though it understood, as though it, too, had grown weary of the struggle and was ready to come out and see what the fuss was about.

"I felt it!" she cried. "I felt it turn over!"

"Yes," he said and set to work helping the little one meet the rest of them.

* * *

It came out deep red and squalling, slippery and warm and wet. Blood never felt so good on Jake's hands as he held it.

"Mad as hell, ain't it?" the old woman said, coming to the side of the bed as Jake held it forth to her. She reached for it and said, "I know what to do from here."

The boy, Frisco, had not moved in all that time, his eyes as big as muffins.

"What is it?" he said.

The old woman looked and said, "It's a baby girl is what it is?"

"What we gone name it?"

The old woman looked at the younger woman.

"What you gone name it?"

"Sadie," the girl said. "Gone name it Sadie."

"Look it all that dark hair on its head," the old woman said.

Jake washed his hands and put on his coat, then came back to the bedside just as the old woman was wrapping the child in a small blanket.

The girl reached for his hand.

"I knew you'd come and save us," she said.

The old woman declared it a "miracle."

"Ain't no miracle, Mama, I seen him come in a dream," she said, her eyes fixed on Jake.

"I know you did, child."

Jake said, "I'll need a ride back to town."

The old woman said, "Frisco, take this good man to town in the wagon."

Then finally the boy stood up and came over next to the bed and looked at the new baby and touched the small dark face.

"Got Chinaman's eyes," he said.

The girl and the old woman laughed.

"They all got Chinaman's eyes when they is first born," the old woman said. "You had 'em, too."

Jake and the boy rode back to town, the boy handling the reins like some old-time freighter.

"How old are you, Frisco?"

"Ten or twelve, I ain't sure exactly."

"I want you to promise me you'll always look after that niece of yours," Jake said when they reached town and he climbed down.

The boy looked at him from under the flop brim of his hat.

"That what she is, a niece to me?"

Jake nodded.

"Niece . . ." the boy said thoughtfully.

"If she'd turned out a boy, it would have been all right with me," he said. "But I'll stand her, I reckon." Jake stood and watched as the boy snapped the reins and turned the wagon back around.

In spite of everything, Jake felt something he hadn't felt in a long time: he felt like a physician again. And for those few hours there with the girl, he did not have to think about the troubles ahead of him, about the fact that he was in essence a man alone once more.

A drink? Why the hell not? It seemed in perfect order. So he went into the Three Aces and had one.

Word had already spread like wildfire that there was a big fight coming between the city marshal and the boys from the Double Bar. And as he stood there alone at the bar drinking, the other drinkers looked sidelong. He heard their mutterings out of the sides of their mouths, but nobody stepped forward and said they'd stand with him. And maybe the truth was, they'd just as soon see something happen with winter now nearly upon them and that long slow season staring them down.

Nobody can save me but me, he thought.

And ordered another drink.

15

❧❦❧

DRUNK, WILLY SILK WAS unceremoniously dumped from the afternoon stage onto the cold and muddy main drag of Sweet Sorrow. The fall startled him and he came to looking at the staring faces of strangers. He saw the way they shook their heads, not in sympathy, but with pity. One woman clucked her tongue, then hove her red-headed child away like a hen herding its chick from potential danger.

The driver of the stage tossed down Willy's kit from the boot of the stage, said, "I believe that is yours," then leaned and spat off to the side.

"Which way to the nearest saloon?" Willy asked, struggling to gain his feet. His gun had fallen out and he bent and picked it up and wiped the mud off with the tail of his shirt.

"Nearest and onliest," the driver said, "is the Three Aces, directly down the street. But was I a guessing man, I'd guess you already have too much liquor in you. Public drunkenness is an abomination. You ought to get straight with the Lord, son."

"Well, you ain't nothing to me, dad," Willy said, sliding the pistol into the hip holster. "And if you was, I'd tell you to mind your own damn business, just as I'm telling you now."

"Pickled," the man said.

"What?"

"You're pickled as an egg. I seen dead men not as pickled as you."

"How'd you like to tell your kin a pickled egg shot you through that big mouth of yours?"

The driver's eyes narrowed.

"You scare me about as much as a garter snake," the driver said, then turned and walked off. Willy watched him go with some small regret that he hadn't stood and chosen to fight it out with guns, for he felt even with killing that old reprobate back in Bismarck, he could still use a little more practice. Then he puked. He straightened and wiped his mouth with the cuff of his sleeve, the bile in the back of his throat burning and raw and in need of washing.

When he got to the Three Aces, he ordered a bottle.

"Glass?" the bartender asked, setting the bottle down on the oak.

"It's something women do," Willy said, "drink out of glasses." He took his bottle over to a table. He sucked a pull from the bottle and felt some little better, but not a lot. Seemed like he couldn't get through a day, even half a day, without numbing his senses with whiskey.

He fashioned himself a smoke and lighted it with a Lucifer struck off the edge of the table, took a deep draw from it before taking a hit from the bottle again, then set it down again. The liquor seemed to take some of the sharp edge off from the long stage ride and temper some of the headache it seemed he'd been suffering ever since he had left Colonel Lily's Wild West Combination three years back. Another thing was he'd had a few blackouts lately and sometimes lost an entire weekend from memory. But mostly it was the damn headaches that got so severe it felt like thumbs were gouging his eyes from the inside out.

Then he caught movement out of the corner of his vision. He could see by the looks of her what she was when she approached the table. She was small ivory-skinned woman who looked to be Oriental, with long black straight hair and dark eyes, and he liked what she looked like, but he wasn't sure he was in the mood for a woman just then.

"My name is Narcissa," she said.

"What you want?" Willy said, testing her a bit, fooling with her because he was in a bad mood and felt like fooling with someone.

She smiled and he could see her teeth weren't the best.

"You buy me drink? I sit with you and we have good time, yes."

Willy looked at the bottle, then at her, before pushing a chair out from the table with his foot.

She sat, he moved the bottle over. She looked around.

"I like drinking from glass," she said.

"It's all right," he said. "Drink from the bottle."

"Okay," she said.

She put the bottle to her lips, but Willy could see she was barely drinking any of it. She set it before him again.

"Now you drink," she said, smiling that fake smile. For behind the eyes he could see a bored dullness that set into every working girl he'd ever met save for one: a whore in Kansas City who had just barely turned seventeen at the time and been put to work by a three-finger pimp named Johnny Lou.

"Sure," Willy said and lifted the bottle to his mouth and took another long pull from it then set it back before the Oriental again. "Now it's your turn."

"We go in back now?" she said.

"How much?"

"Ten dollar," she said, reaching across the table with her hand.

He drew on the smoke, then exhaled.

"Ten, huh?"

She nodded.

He could see another whore standing at the bar, talking to a man with red garters on his shirtsleeves. The whore kept glancing over at the table where Willy and the Chinese girl sat.

Willy reached into his pocket, saw that his roll was getting skinny. Take two for the bottle, ten for the whore. It would eat most of his poke.

"No," he said. "Maybe later."

She put on a pout.

"I give it to you for less?" she said, starting to stand.

He shook his head.

"Sit down and drink some more with me," he ordered.

The whore at the bar came over and stood next to the China girl.

"He giving you trouble?" she said, looking straight at Willy.

Willy looked up at her, said, "Why is any of this your business?"

The white whore had rouged cheeks and a mole near the side of her mouth. She had pocked skin. She looked like death and murder. Willy saw her reaching into the pocket of her skirt.

"Don't," he said.

Her hand paused.

"You think I wouldn't shoot a woman?" Willy said. "Well, you'd be wrong."

"A real gentleman, huh," she said.

"Damn straight," Willy said sourly.

The white one was older, had a small moon-shaped scar under her chin. Something about her made Willy want her more than the Oriental and made him think whatever the cost he was going to have her, one way or the other—maybe just to prove he could.

"How much for you?" Willy said.

"Go to hell," she said and turned and took the Oriental by the arm and pulled her away and toward the bar.

Willy took another pull on the whiskey and watched them, then took another draw on his cigarette.

This man he was looking for, this—he took the wanted poster out of his pocket and unfolded it and spread it out there on the table—this Tristan Shade. His eyes scanned the room, the air sooty, and he looked over the boys there drinking and didn't see that any of them resembled this fellow. He reached back and scratched up under his hat. His scalp itched and it would be no surprise if he had caught the cooties off that stage seat or somewhere else. He hadn't bathed in a week or better, hadn't shaved in nearly as long. He felt grungy and unsettled, but somehow it really didn't matter, he told himself. He just didn't give a damn that much about it.

He studied the likeness drawn on the poster for a long and hard spell before putting it back again in his pocket. *Doctor, huh?* He took another pull from the bottle. He

saw the two whores talking to some men down at the far
end of the bar, saw the way the one looked back at him—
the older ugly white one—with that pitted face and that
scar on her chin and those pitiless eyes.

Hell, he thought, *it don't get no better than this.*

16

⊰≎⊱

THE FLESH OF ELLIS KANSAS had become putrid. Jake took the bandage from around the saloon keeper's neck, smelled rottenness almost the same time he saw the ugly wound. *Infected.* He found a bottle of carbolic acid and cleaned the nasty gunshot flesh, then put on a clean bandage. Fever had set in. Kansas rolled his eyes, then closed them.

In the parlor Clara stood looking out at the snow through a double set of leaded windows. The snow fell softly, silently. Winter was finally upon them. She stood with her arms crossed, holding herself, while her daughters played in the snow, trying to build a snowman, and it reminded her of a time when she was a little girl and the sight of her father's coal black moustache crusted with ice as he helped her.

Jake said, "He's dying."

Clara turned.

"No," she said.

Jake came and stood at the window.

He stood close to her and she wanted him to take her in his arms, to reassure her somehow that the world would be right again—that such violent acts as what happened to the saloon keeper would somehow go away and never return.

"I've got a problem, Clara."

She looked up at him, saw that his gaze followed that of the children.

"What is it?" she said.

"Some men are going to come and kill me."

He did not look at her when he said that, but if he had he would have seen the effect it had on her.

"Then you have to run," she said.

"I thought about it."

But she could tell by the sound of his voice he'd made a decision not to.

"Who are these men, Jake?"

"Some ranch hands from the Double Bar," he said. "They know I know they were the ones who killed that Negro cowboy and they know I'm going to arrest them."

She took in a deep breath, let it out, then moved against him, pushing her body against his, and he put his arm around her.

"Don't stay," she said. "I'm pleading with you to leave."

"No guarantee that even if I run they wouldn't pursue me."

His hands reached up and felt the cool damp thickness of her hair. She'd been washing it in a deep pan when he'd arrived; one of the girls had let him in, saying, "Mama's washing her hair with melted snow water in the kitchen." He brought it to his face and it smelled like morning in a meadow after a rain. Her face was warm and flush and her mouth tender when he kissed her and he thought there is nothing as sweet as a woman with fresh-washed hair.

"What will you do?" she said softly.

The snow seemed to dance on the thin gray air as it tumbled earthward. The girls ran about, flopping down and pouncing on each other like kittens, then scrambling to their feet again, remembering the task they'd set for themselves of building a snowman. When Clara looked at them, her heart filled with pride. But her heart was full of sorrow, too, hearing this news: that Mr. Ellis was dying, that men were coming to kill the man she knew she was falling in love with—the man who she could never openly say those words to because he'd given no indication that he felt the same toward her.

"Stand and fight is my only choice," he said.

"What about the others? Won't they stand with you. Have you asked them?"

"They won't stand," he said. "Maybe John will, but . . ."

"Jake, I need to say this, even though I know you probably don't want to hear it. I need to say it." It wasn't something she'd planned on revealing.

He turned his gaze from the playing children, the snow, the endless white landscape, and rested it on her. He saw in her face a place of sanctuary if he wanted it, he saw in her eyes the offer of some future hope if he wanted it. He saw beauty that springs from a woman with an honest heart.

"Jake, I'll go with you. Me and the girls. We'll leave together and we'll find a place and make a home together. I . . ."

He took her face in his hands.

"I can't let you get in the middle of this, Clara."

"No, damn it! I want to be in the middle of it if it means saving you."

Her eyes brimmed and he drew her into him and held her tightly until the small sobs of regret and sorrow subsided.

"I would give my life to protect you, Clara, just as you're offering to give yours for me. But this is not something I can allow you to do." He looked out at the children again, saw how happy their red faces were, could hear their muted laughter. He thought of Ellis back there alone, dying, and how death comes to men unbidden, suddenly, striking like a snake or black lightning, striking down whomever it calls upon without warning or discretion. It was almost as though such men as Ellis and Nat Pickett had been standing in line, one after the other, waiting their turn to walk through death's black door, a door that they all must eventually pass through. And now he was next in line and it was his turn to meet that mysterious event.

He kissed her lightly on the mouth and fought his desire to be more intimate with her, for the snow was falling and the children outside playing and blissful and unaware of what was transpiring inside the house. The rooms were empty and cool, except for the one where Ellis Kansas lay dying. It would have been easy just to go off to one of the rooms with her, just for a short time. She kissed him back, more passionately, more needy, as though it was the last kiss they'd share. And maybe it was.

But instead he separated himself from her and said simply, "I need to go, Clara."

She clung to his arms a moment longer, then released him as she might a kite caught by the wind that had been tugging on the string she held. And like a kite caught on the wind, she watched him take his leave, go out and pause there by the children, who looked up at him, their coats caked with snow, and their mittens as well. And he knelt between them and wrapped his arms around each of them and drew them into him and whispered something to them, then stood again and trudged off toward town.

She wept openly. The girls—her little girls—stared after him for the longest time, then went back to being kittens.

The ride to Toussaint's seemed to take longer than usual. Maybe it was the silence of riding through the snow, only occasionally broken by the snuffle of the horse, the jingle of bit, the creak of cold saddle leather. Once he could hear the caw of crows somewhere but couldn't actually see them. The cottonwoods along Cooper's Creek off in the distance looked black, foreboding, like shreds of mourning crepe hanging from some invisible window.

The little house stood bleak against the wintry landscape. A smudge of smoke curled from the stovepipe, poking through the roof at one end. Beyond a short ways he could see the lone stone that marked the grave of their boy, Dex, under a cap of snow. He drew in at the house and tied off the horse, then knocked on the door, stamping snow off his boots and sweeping it off the brim of his hat.

Karen answered. She beamed when she saw him and he was just as pleased to see her again so soon, but his mission was a troubled one and he knew he had to keep it from her if he could.

"Married life suits you, Karen," he said as she hugged him.

Their adopted son, Stephen, came and took his hat and he rubbed the boy's thin blond hair, saying, "You're getting big as your pa."

From the back part of the house he could hear Toussaint.

"If it's that damn drummer, run him off!"

Karen shook her head.

"He's cranky," she said. "Some drummer came

around selling Bibles the other day. They weighed five pounds each, it felt like. I thought about buying one, but Toussaint said we'd be wasting our money. Said, 'There ain't nothing in it but fairy tales.' I don't know what to do with the man." This she said with the warm soft humor of a woman in love.

Then she said, "He broke his leg. It doesn't help his mood."

Toussaint appeared in the door, leaning on a homemade crutch made from the branch of a tree.

"Oh," he said. "I thought you were that Bible drummer. I was going to pitch you into the snow."

Jake held up his hands.

"No Bibles."

Toussaint hobbled over to the table and sat down heavily, awkwardly, keeping his left leg out straight. Jake could see there was a homemade splint around it as well: two wood rods that looked like sawed off broom handles—which is exactly what they were—tied with strips of muslin.

"When did you do that?" Jake asked, nodding toward the leg. "I mean, you didn't have it the other day when we were out here."

"We got any coffee?" Toussaint said to Karen, as though he hadn't even heard the question.

She said, "He fell off a horse."

"Fell, hell, got thrown off that hammerhead."

"We went horse hunting and caught three and my wild cowboy here said he'd green-break them for me, that we'd get a few extra dollars if they were green-broke. I said, 'You don't know nothing about breaking horses. You don't even like riding them,' but he didn't listen. He climbed on the back of that rough buckskin out yonder in the corral and it pitched him. That's how it happened."

Toussaint swallowed as though he had a crabapple stuck in his throat and said, "I guess a man could grow old and die around here waiting for a simple cup of coffee."

Karen wiped her hands on her apron and set about brewing a pot of coffee. The boy came and sat next to Toussaint and looked at him, then the stiff leg, and said, "Does it hurt, Pa?"

"Course it hurts, boy. Broken bones is gone to hurt, just hope you don't ever find out how much. You do your arithmetic lessons?"

"Yes, Pa. And my reading lessons, too."

"What about your Latin?"

The boy looked sheepish.

Toussaint looked like he wanted to say something else about it, but he couldn't think of what it was he wanted to say, so instead he begrudgingly said, "I think there still might be some hard candy back there in my tin box. But just once piece or else your ma will get all over me for spoiling you."

The boy grew a smile and went off to find the candy. Toussaint's gaze followed him and Jake could see the pride in those dark eyes. But it was also a pride that bordered on sorrow for the other son that was not among them—the one that lay under the cold ground out back of the house.

"What brings you out here?" Toussaint said, turning his attention back to Jake.

"There's something I want to talk to you about." Jake saw Karen turn her head around to look at them from where she stood at the stove. Jake waited till she turned back around, then slanted his eyes toward the door for Toussaint's benefit. "Some private business."

Toussaint looked at his wife's back. He could tell she was listening and interested in whatever it was Jake wanted to tell him. He stood, got the crutch under his arm, and said to Karen, "I could use some help getting my coat on. I got to go check on the horses."

"I can check on them," she said. "You go out in that snow one-legged, you'll just fall on your can and bust your other leg, then you won't be a bit of use to me and I'll just have to take that old gun and do to you what I'd do to an old dog that had gone rabid. I'd just as soon not be put through all the trouble. It'd be easier was I to check the horses myself."

"Fine, take the boy with you. He needs to learn to take care of his animals."

"He already knows how," she said. "But I'll take him anyway, because I'd not want you and Jake here to have to talk your man talk around women and children."

"I apologize, Karen," Jake said. "I just want to ask Toussaint a little advice on a personal matter."

She turned and with a genuine smile said, "Don't mind me, Jake. I'm just a little testy when it comes to him. Lord knows, we all been through enough this last year." And she looked at Toussaint with unhidden love.

"Don't worry, woman," Toussaint said softly. "You know you and that boy come first with me. Now let us have a second, if you would."

She got her and the boy's coat and helped him on with it and they went out. A breath of cold air came in when they opened the door; the fire in the stove ate it.

"So what's the deal?" Toussaint said when they were alone.

Jake told him.

Toussaint listened, then said, "How can I help?"

Jake looked down at the leg.

"You can't," he said.

" 'Cause of this? Shit."

"No, because of them," Jake said. Toussaint looked at the door as though he could see out into the yard, clear out to the corral where Karen and the boy had gone.

"They'll understand. Karen will, anyway."

"Not if you are brought home wrapped in a tarp, they won't."

"Karen's a tough woman," Toussaint said.

"I really just want to know one thing: If it was you, how would you handle it, considering the circumstances?"

Toussaint rubbed his leg up high where it ached, where the pain had gone from the lower part where the bone was broken, as though the pain had to find another place to settle.

"I'd kill them before they were ready to be killed," Toussaint said.

"What's that mean?"

"I wouldn't wait for them to come after me. I'd go after them and I'd kill them in their sleep if I had to or any other way I could find them."

"I can't do that," Jake said.

"Why not?"

"Because I can't. It's not in me to do something like that."

"Then they will kill you just as bad and merciless as they did that colored cowboy. Sure, you might get one or two if you're lucky and they come at you straight on. But they're not going to come at you straight on because they know you'll be ready for them. My advice, if you don't want to die, is get in the wind."

"I'm not running—not from them, I'm not."

Toussaint had a pained look on his face.

"Not one of those sons a bitches in town will stand with you?"

Jake shook his head.

"Just John, but I can't ask him; he's not made of fighting stock, not like you."

"You could wire down to Bismarck and see if they'll send some lawmen to help you out on this."

"No," Jake said. "I can't do that either." The last thing Jake needed were lawmen who might have a dodger on him.

Toussaint nodded knowingly.

" 'Cause you're on the dodge yourself . . ."

"Something like that. It's a long story. Someday I'll tell you about it."

They both knew that the odds were likely Jake would never get that chance.

"You say the word, and I'll get my damn shotgun," Toussaint said. "Hell, I don't need both legs to shoot with."

"Appreciate it," Jake said. "But Karen needs you and that little boy needs you a lot worse than I do."

They both knew it was true.

"Besides, what would it look like, me having a one-legged man in a gunfight."

Jake tried to play it off light, but Toussaint didn't smile.

"There's a lot better places to die than here in Sweet Sorrow," Toussaint said. "And a lot better ways than what you're facing if you stay."

"Yeah," Jake said. "I don't doubt that there are."

Toussaint hobbled to the door as Jake went out. Jake met Karen and the boy by the corral. Toussaint watched the lawman stop and give her a hug, then pat the boy on the shoulder before mounting his horse and riding off.

Karen came and said, "So you want to tell me what it was he wanted?"

"He wanted to say good-bye, is all."

"Men," she said. "I'll never understand what it is about you all that makes you want to keep secrets. Get ready for dinner."

Toussaint looked down at the boy. The boy looked up at him. Out in the corral the horses nickered. They were restless, he figured, wanting to be free to run like they had been before he and Karen had ridden out and threw ropes around their necks and penned them up. He looked at the rough buckskin filly that had thrown him into the fence and broke his leg, watched the way she circled around in the corral, looking for an escape route. She stopped and looked at him across the distance—her large eyes dark and wet. She snuffled and tossed her mane. She snorted steam. He thought about Jake and those damn boys from the Double Bar and what would happen when they all came together. Then he turned and went back inside and closed the door and sat down at the table again and drank his coffee, feeling miserable.

It was like that time he found Dex shot dead in the grass. Something he hated and ate at his guts, but couldn't do any damn thing about it, like now. It came down to a choice between his own family and the lawman.

What was it that Bible drummer had said?

Trust in Jesus.

Well, Jesus would have to be a fool to wander out onto these prairies unless he had a pistol and knew well how to use it. Because one thing was certain: those Double Bar boys didn't care nothing about Jesus, or the law or nothing else.

Karen said, "You want more coffee?"

"Please," he said.

But later she saw he never drank it, just let it sit there and grow cold.

"Whatever it is he wanted of you," she said, "I know you'd do it. And if you feel it's something you have to do, go ahead. But I have to say this one thing: I couldn't stand it if something was to happen to you—but I'd make it through. That boy, though, I'm not sure he could take losing another daddy."

She wasn't sure if he'd heard her or not. He never acted like he did or didn't. He just sat there with his cup of coffee growing cold.

17

❧❧

THE BUNKHOUSE WAS LONG and low-slung, made of logs dragged in from farther north. Nobody bothered scraping the bark off them. They were notched and chinked with mud and shakes were cut for the roof and there was stovepipes—one at either end—fed by small potbellies that heated the interior during the cold months and in between there was a space where cold air lingered and the boys never sat in the middle but closer to the stoves.

Along one wall was a row of bunks with tick mattresses and on each bed were two blankets wove of wool. Some of the hands kept their personals in small trunks they set at the end of their bunks and others kept their things in saddle bags hung over the head of the beds or wrapped up in their soogins they kept underneath their bunks. They hung stiff lariats and their chaps on pegs along the opposite wall. There was a long table with spoke-back chairs they pulled up close to one of the stoves in the cold months and took outside to eat off of in the warm months. A pair of bull's-eye lanterns sat on the table and a deck of worn playing cards, and somebody had at one time or another left a checkerboard there, but some of the checkers had been lost over time, so when the boys played the game, they used Mexican pesos to replace the missing pieces because you couldn't spend a Mexican peso in any of the local establishments. One of the boys had been down in the border town of Neuvo Laredo and that's where the pesos had come from.

Dallas and Perk sat across from each other. Taylor, Harvey, and Lon sat along the table down from them. Taylor was stitching a hole in the elbow of a shirt, and Lon and Harvey were just smoking.

"When we gone do it?" Perk said, his crazy eyes moving back and forth.

"When I say is when," Dallas said.

The others listened without speaking.

"What we waiting for?" Perk said. "Why don't we do it and get over and done with?"

"I want him to sweat some," Dallas said. He took out his makings, which were near empty—the sack having maybe enough for one more smoke in it—and shook the tobacco into a paper he'd grooved, then rolled up, licking along one edge, then twisting off the ends.

"Longer he has to think about it, the more nervous he's gone be. That's how I want him."

Perk picked at a scab on the back of his wrist.

"Longer he has to plan on us coming, too."

Dallas lit the shuck and took a draw off it, then let the smoke curl out of his mouth, some of it climbing up into his eyes. He had the weathered face of a man who'd spent most of his life on horseback and doing outdoor work. He had the look of a man who'd met a lot of disappointment in his life.

He looked from Perk to the others.

"You all with me on this?"

Taylor tugged at the end of the thread with his teeth trying to bite it off. He shrugged and said, "You're the one who's a planner, Dallas. Ain't none of us planners much. You want to wait and go in later, that suits me."

"How 'bout you?" Dallas said, looking at Lon and Harvey.

They shrugged as well.

"Fine by me," Lon said.

"Fine by me, too," Harvey said.

Then they all just sat there for a time, Dallas and them smoking, Taylor examining the stitched hole in the elbow of his shirt. He shook it out and held it up. It had been washed so many times it had grown thin over time. He could see light through it. It was a shirt he wore only now and then, on special occasions, like when he got duded up to go into town and drink and get with whores.

Perk stood away from the table and went to one of the two small windows cut into either end of the bunkhouse to let some light in and rubbed frost away with the heel of his hand and looked out.

"It's snowing to beat the band," he said.

Nobody said anything.

"I guess was we to ride in there today and kill that son of a bitch, it would be tough going just to get there and back. Snow's piling up like the dead at Gettysburg."

Perk had fought in the war, had been at Gettysburg. He'd seen the way men got shot down and stacked up one atop the other in some places—the cornfield, for one. He saw them afterward, too, in the heat, several days later, their bodies swollen tight inside their clothes. He remembered how death smelled, like it was yesterday he'd smelled it. It had made him want never to be in a hot country again. He liked winter. He liked the way it looked, the snow laying deep in white drifts. He liked the

sound of his boots crunching in it, liked the taste of it
even. Most of all, he liked its clean silence.

Lon and Harvey set up the checkerboard, Lon taking
the black pieces and Harvey the red, and using the Mexican pesos for the missing pieces.

"Smoke before fire," Harvey said and Lon moved
first.

Dallas watched them for a time, then stood up and
went out the door and trudged to the privy and dropped
his drawers and sat down on the cold wood there in the
dark little house with bands of light filtering through the
cracks. He sat there until he was finished, then he buttoned up and went out again. The snow fell slantways directly into his face and he had to squint. He had been
thinking about the girl, the baby in her, was it his or not
his. It made his insides clinch up like a fist to think maybe
it was not his, that it was Nat's kid in her.

*How's a white woman have any truck with a damn
coon?*

He trudged to the corral and looked at the horses,
their shaggy coats grown thick already, their eyes black
in their heads, their black noses wet. They had small
blankets of snow on their backs.

Inside the cabin Perk was watching Dallas standing
there at the corral, thinking, *That's the meanest son of a
bitch I ever knew.* Then, after a while of watching, he
went over near the stove and held out his hands, rubbing
them. His feet were cold and he pulled a chair up and
straightened out his legs so the soles of his boots were
near the hot iron. He thought about Nat Pickett. All he
could see was Nat's big smile, those white teeth in that
dark face, how Nat was always quick to laugh at everything and had about him the ways of a kid, always

pulling pranks, but never going too far with them because he knew the boys wouldn't tolerate all that much from a nigger, even if he was a good hand. About the only one who showed him any deference was Tig. They were somewhat alike in their ways—both of 'em always looking at life as though it was a joke. But it wasn't any joke. Life was hard most of the time, nothing but hard work and ornery horses and too little pay and cheap whiskey and women who only loved you until your money run out. The life of a cowhand was never having no real home and drifting from one place to the next, because you got fired or got tired of it all and quit. Boys like Tig and Nat didn't understand such things yet 'cause they were too young to understand them. They didn't know nothing about the old ways, about hard and war and such.

Perk could smell the leather of his boots after a time from the heat. It wasn't an unpleasant smell.

Bob Parker came out of the house and he saw his man, Dallas, standing over at the corral looking at the horses, and went over to him and said, "There something wrong?" He looked at the horses, too, but he couldn't see anything wrong with any of them.

Dallas had one foot resting on the bottom rail and his forearms resting on the top and he was just staring at the horses and said, "No, they ain't nothing wrong."

"I want to know something," Bob Parker said, sort of resting on the railings, too. The air was cold and sharp and he could smell the horses, that sweet scent they had about them, a smell he'd always liked since the first time he smelled them.

Dallas didn't ask what it was the boss wanted to know, just stood there, looking, his breath coming in frosty regularity.

"I want to know did you have anything to do with that boy's death?"

Dallas's mouth moved, like he had something stuck in his teeth and was trying to pry it out with his tongue. He finally turned his head and looked directly into Bob Parker's face and said, "Goddamn you, to ask me a thing like that."

Bob Parker shifted his bulk. He was a good head taller than Dallas and forty pounds heavier. He didn't know for sure what Dallas might do next. He braced himself, just in case, but told himself he'd whip that rascal seven ways from Sunday if he tried anything.

"It's my place, and that boy was my hand, and I guess I got a right to ask any questions I want to as long as you're working for me, collecting wages out of my pocket."

The cold had burned color into Dallas's hollow cheeks and his nose.

He spit over the top rail into the muddy horse-tromped paddock.

"I ain't even going to answer something like that," Dallas said, then removed his foot from the lower rail and turned to walk off.

Bob Parker said, "This is my place, not yours. I seen what you did to Tig, you and the others. You can't be riding roughshod over these boys . . ."

Dallas stopped short and turned and looked at his boss, the snow falling down between them. They were maybe twenty paces apart, about as far as you'd want a man to be from you if you were going to shoot him with a handgun.

"He tell you it was me hurt him like that?"

"He didn't say if it was or it wasn't. He didn't say

nothing, but that he wanted his pay. But he sure didn't get like that by no accident, either."

Dallas knew he'd have to unbutton his coat to get at the pistol he wore. And he could do it, for he didn't see where Bob Parker had come armed. It'd be easy if he wanted to. But he knew Bob to be well-respected in this country and killing him might just raise a lynch mob unless he could cover his tracks well enough. 'Sides, there were those other boys to worry about if he was just to shoot Bob down—would they back him on it or turn tail and maybe even turn witness against him if it came down to it? Killing that colored Nat was one thing, but Bob Parker was a white man and he didn't know if Taylor and them would stand up for it or not like they did with the killing of Nat.

"That's a hell of a thing to accuse me of, boss. I mean, it's a hell of a thing. I guess if you go to accusing a man of something like that, you got to be prepared for the consequences. I don't guess nobody would blame me was I to stand up for myself, you calling me a liar and all. That's the same as calling a man out round this country."

Bob Parker saw the predicament he'd put himself in. He hadn't come out armed and he knew Dallas never went anywhere without one. He could see the bulge of Dallas's pistol there under his coat. He felt his nerve failing him a little. Knew he'd stepped into it.

"I mean, if you want to accuse me of something like that, I guess I'd just have to stand up for myself," Dallas said again, a harder edge to his voice as his fingers stiffly undid the lower buttons of his coat.

Bob held up a hand.

"I don't guess I'm accusing you of nothing just yet," he said.

"Well, that's good, boss."

Just then a shrill voice came from the house.

"Bob!"

It was his wife calling.

Dallas looked past his boss toward the house, could barely make her out there in the doorway with the snow falling hard as it was between them.

"You better go on, boss. Better go see what it is your wife wants," Dallas said.

"I ain't armed," Bob said.

"Yeah, well, you better just go on before this all gets out of hand."

He watched as Bob Parker backed up a few steps, then turned and walked toward the house. He made an easy target.

"What's he doing?" Taylor said, having set down his mended shirt and gone over to the window and rubbed the glass with the heel of his hand, then looked out in time to see Dallas standing by the corral, him and the boss, facing each other. "Looks like he's *arging* with the boss."

"Them two never were very friendly," Lon said. He was up in the game of checkers. Harvey never could think very far ahead on the moves to stay even with him.

Perk looked up from his stiff boots that had grown hot on the soles.

"They's liable to go at it one of these days. Old Bob better watch his step."

"Looks like they almost just did," Taylor said. "Only the boss is walking off toward the house now."

"Is it still snowing out there?" Lon said.

"Yes. Snowing like hell."

"He coming back in?"

"No, he's getting his saddle. Looks like he's gone ride off somewheres."

"Ride off?"

"Looks like."

Perk stood up, the soles of his boots curled hard from the heat, and shuffled over to the window and looked out, too. Dallas had slipped between the rails and tossed a rope over the neck of a roan and was putting his saddle on it.

"Where you reckon he's riding off to?" Taylor said.

"I don't have a clue."

"You think he's gone ride into town and shoot that lawman by himself?"

"No, it ain't his way."

"Why not, as mean a mean son of a bitch as he is?"

"He ain't gone take no chances," Perk said. "I don't think. Dallas is smart in that way."

The snow seemed to let up some, just as Dallas swung aboard the roan and rode it over to the gate and leaned and slipped off the loop of wire holding it, then rode out neatly and replaced it over the post as the other horses watched.

"No, he's gone the other way from town," Taylor said.

"Out to where that girl is living, I bet he's going," Perk said.

"That one Nat got knocked up."

Perk looked at Taylor.

"You don't know it was him."

"Could be it's Dallas's kid in her."

"I guess we'll all know when it comes out," Lon said, and he triple-jumped Harvey's last three men, including the Mexican pesos, and said, "That's it, you lose again."

Harvey sat there looking at the board.

"Shit," he said.

Lon scratched up under his hat in the back and tilted it forward so it set low over his eyes and a grin spread across his mouth.

"You want to play again?"

"Okay, but this time I'll take the black ones."

"That kid comes out colored," Taylor said, "Dallas may shoot that girl."

"He might," Perk said. "It wouldn't surprise me none."

Then they moved away from the window and went and sat at the table and watched the checker game.

18

J AKE WAS THERE IN THE SALOON when the commotion
began. He had arrived back in Sweet Sorrow under a
dark red sky. Evening came early that time of year and
his journey from Toussaint's had been slowed consider-
ably by the snow that in places had drifted as deep as his
horse's belly.

He did not know what awaited him upon his return:
whether or not the boys from the Double Bar would be
there waiting for him, armed and ready to gun him
down. He had thought over both Toussaint and Clara's
advice to run. It would be easy to swing the horse north,
cross the border, and to hell with everything. But if he
found trouble in a far-flung settlement like Sweet Sorrow,
there was no assurance that he wouldn't find more of it
some other place as well. And what would he do each
time he found it, or it found him? Run? No. Comes a
time when a man has to stand his ground and take trouble head on. Wearily, he thought that if he had stayed in
Denver and faced a trial of his peers, he possibly could
have proven to them that it wasn't him who had killed
Shaw—his lover's husband—but *her*. But he did not then

trust his fate to a jury of his peers, and his fear had won out and he had run. And now he knew what it felt like to have quit the fight and he didn't ever want to have to feel that way again, even if it meant he might lose his life. *There are some things worth dying for*, he concluded.

So he did not turn the horse north, but rode on to Sweet Sorrow, a place he had come to consider home, if there was ever to be such a thing for him, and when he saw the town's lights twinkling in the rosy dusk, he was glad to see them and rode straight to the Fat Duck Café for some hot coffee and a meal.

He sat alone, even though there were others there he knew. Nobody greeted him; he'd become a pariah to them because of the impending trouble with the Double Bar boys and nobody wanted to get in the middle of it. He couldn't blame them. And he didn't.

Fannie came around with coffee. They seemed as complete strangers now. *Funny*, he thought, *how two people can share the intimacy we had that one time and end up feeling like strangers to each other*. She was cordial in the way that a waitress is supposed to be cordial.

She poured him a cup of coffee and said, "Have you decided what you'll have?"

He looked up at her, but she had a distant look in her eyes.

"I'll have the stew," he said.

She started to turn toward the kitchen.

"How's everything with you?" he said.

"Everything's fine, Marshal."

"You and Will Bird getting on okay?"

It was a strange thing to ask her, he knew. But right then he felt like he could use some friendly conversation and thought it might lead to such.

She looked at him then for the first real time and he

could see there was still some old jealousy there because he hadn't taken up with her when he could have, that he had turned her down and now she'd found herself another man, someone who *did* want her.

"Will and me are getting along just fine," she said, then turned and walked to the kitchen.

He looked around at the tables of other diners. The place itself was long and narrow, squeezed between the barbershop and the dentist's office. The German had a stamped tin ceiling set in and painted green and the walls were eggshell white down to the wainscoting. The flooring was four-inch-wide oak planks and the tables were covered with checkered tablecloths. In the back was the kitchen, where the German did the cooking and baking, and you could smell the foods, the kraut especially, which he cooked in large pots, and the breads he baked, too.

Jake drank his coffee and stared out the window there, just inside the front door where he'd taken the only vacant table left because most did not like sitting near the door in the winter when every opening and closing let in blasts of cold air. Droplets of moisture clung to the windows.

He felt a deep, deep weariness and when Fannie brought his plate of stew, he ate it slowly, letting the warmth sink down into him, warming his belly, and he sipped his coffee slowly, too. And when he finished, he put a silver dollar on the table—seventy-five cents for the stew, a nickel for the coffee, and a twenty-cent tip—then stood and put on his hat and buttoned his coat and went out and down the street to the saloon, where he ordered a glass of whiskey and was drinking it when the commotion began.

The girl came running into the main room—one of Ellis Kansas's working girls. She had blood on her right hand and somebody grabbed hold of her—another working girl, a Chinese—and their screams cut through the din.

Jake moved away from the bar, unbuttoning his coat as he did, thinking if he had to get to his pistol . . .

"What's going on here?" he said to the girl.

She looked at him.

"He tried to kill me."

"Who?"

She pointed toward the back, where the girls took their customers.

Jake drew his pistol and said, "You wait here."

It happened so fast Willy Silk didn't have time to think before he realized he'd been stabbed. The girl's knife went in just below his ribs, where his kidneys were. He'd been sitting there on the edge of the bed taking off his boots, his thoughts garbled, floating on the sea of whiskey he'd drunk. He never thought twice about it when she'd come around him the second time and asked him if he wanted to go to the back.

He said to her, "I thought you didn't like me."

"Why is that?" she'd said, sitting down at his table.

" 'Cause of the way you acted with me and that China girl."

She laughed and said, "Oh that, that wasn't nothing. I was just putting on a front. I didn't want her to have you. I wanted you for myself."

He looked at her, that pocked face, and that little bone white scar under her chin. He'd wished it silently and now here she was—this ugly whore who had intrigued him.

"Maybe that China girl could join us," he said.

She maintained her smile and said, "Narcissa is with

another customer right now. But maybe when she's finished . . ."

"How much?" he said.

"Don't worry about it," she said. "We'll work something out." He should have known, but he was already drunk and nothing made sense to him anyhow.

Then they were walking to the back together and he had his arm around her shoulder and she was saying, "It's just right back down here." They walked down a narrow hall with doors on either side and she led him into one and said, "Why don't you go ahead and get undressed."

So he sat down on the side of the bed and began pulling off his boots and that's when he felt the sudden stinging pain and reached around just as she pulled the blade out of him and stepped back. It didn't seem like all that much at first, but then he saw the amount of blood on his hand where he'd reached around and a second later he felt himself sliding off the bed to his knees. Then it felt like a fire spreading throughout his entire body and the pain turned crippling.

"What'd you do that for?"

She just stood there looking at him, the knife still in her hand.

"You men are all stinking bastards!" she said.

He fell over onto his side then, the pain catching real hold, eating him up, it felt like.

"I stuck you good, you son of a bitch," she said.

He felt sick. Then he wretched all that whiskey he'd been drinking and it burned in his throat when it came up again. Jesus Christ, he'd never felt such pain.

The room was small. Just a small bed against the wall with a lavender spread. The walls were bare except plaster and cracking in places and up in one corner he could

see where it had rained once and water had come through
and stained it. A crucifix hung above the bed. The yellow
light from a lamp on a nightstand just below it shone upward with eerie effect. There wasn't even a window. The
floor was bare and cold underneath him and he pressed
his face to it to try and cool himself down a little because
he was hotter than hell. Everything had the smell of sex
and blood to it and something ominous passed through
him like a cloud passing before the sun, cutting off the
light.

Then he heard her go out and shut the door behind her.

Jake tried the doors until he came to the one with the man
lying on the floor. He took the lamp from near the bed and
brought it down close and saw the pool of blood underneath him. The back of the man's clothing was wet with
blood. He had one boot on and the other off lying nearby.

The man was groaning.

"What happened here?" Jake said.

The man gritted his teeth.

"That bitch stabbed me, is what . . ." he said.

Others had come and gathered in the doorway—men
who'd been drinking in the main bar and had heard the
woman's story and had come to set things right, to bring
some sort of frontier justice to a man who would assault
a woman; whore or no whore, a woman was still held in
high esteem and in short supply. Jake could hear them behind him muttering their displeasure with "any son of a
bitch who would rough up a woman!"

Jake lifted away the man's shirt and saw the stab
wound. Saw the blood spilling from it, dark and copious.
The blade may have gone into a kidney.

Beneath the scraggly beard, the man appeared young,

but he was ill-kempt and smelled of liquor and sweat. He wasn't someone he'd seen around Sweet Sorrow before. There were growing grumblings of wanting to take the fellow outside and teach him a lesson.

"This man's near dead, I need some help carrying him over to Doc's place."

Nobody stepped forward.

"Gus, get your ass in here."

Gus Boone stepped sheepishly into the room.

"Take his ankles," Jake said.

Gus looked around.

"But Marshal . . ."

"Take his ankles!"

The sometimes jailer, sometimes town drunk did as he was ordered and together they carried Willy Silk over to Clara's, into the rear entrance where the late Doc Willis kept his office and infirmary and where that very moment Ellis Kansas lay with a blood poison and himself fighting off death.

They laid Willy Silk on the exam table on his side and Jake lighted several lamps and brought them in close. Clara had heard them from the parlor and now entered the room.

"What can I do to help?" she said as soon as she saw the blood.

Jake told her while Gus shrank back and then eased himself out the side door. And as he walked back to the saloon, he could see dark splotches of blood in the snow; it reminded him of when he used to kill chickens for a living and how their blood would be everywhere and it made him a little sick to look at it.

And later, after Jake had cleaned and stitched the wound, he and Clara sat in the kitchen across from each other. She'd gotten down a decanter of sherry and poured them each some and said finally, "Is he going to die, too?"

Jake looked toward the door that led back to the infirmary and said, "I don't know, but there is that possibility."

"How did it happen?"

"You don't really want the details, Clara."

"You think that I'm too fragile to know such things?" she said.

"Maybe so. It's enough of a burden to you that I have to use your house for a hospital."

"I wouldn't have this house if it hadn't been for you."

She didn't have to remind him of the fact that he'd been instrumental in trying to save her dying father, the famed gunman, William Sunday, and that it was Sunday who had given him the money for her to buy the house.

"It was over a woman," Jake said. "Something between him and one of the whores at the Three Aces. I don't know exactly what yet."

Clara poured them each a bit more sherry and drew her shawl tighter around her shoulders.

"Jake. I'm afraid for you. It is as though dreadful things are happening all around you and you're doing your best to stave them off, but in the end you won't be able to. In the end I am afraid that some men will carry *you* in the back door and lay you on the table and I'll have to see you like that—like those poor men back there—maybe even worse . . ."

She fought back the tears.

"Let's not worry about things that haven't happened, Clara."

"I can't not worry about them."

"Can I ask you something?"

She nodded.

"Do you believe in fate? That whatever is meant to happen will happen, irregardless of what we do?"

"I don't know, Jake. Sometimes I do, sometimes I don't. I don't think you are fated to die because of those cowboys. I think you can choose to run and save yourself, if that's what you mean."

"No," he said. "I can't choose that. I think whatever is going to happen is going to happen, no matter if I stay or run."

She rose and came to him and put her arms around him and drew his head to her bosom and held him like a mother might a child and he felt her strength pass into him, it seemed, and he said, "I'm so damn tired, Clara."

"I know you are, Jake," she whispered.

And while the snow fell quietly outside, she led him again to her room.

"I should go," he said.

"No."

And with the gentlest care she undressed him and then herself and brought her warmth and strength into the bed next to him. And they lay holding each other beneath the heavy quilt.

He said, "Wake me early, so I can be gone before the girls get up and find us."

"Don't worry about them," she said. "Just sleep, my love."

He closed his eyes. He felt her warm sweet breath on his shoulder.

"Just sleep," she whispered.

And for that moment the world seemed as peaceful as it looked under the mantel of snow, there in the quiet darkness of a red sky and the winking of lights along Main Street.

As though the world, too, was exhausted and wanting to sleep.

19

❖

HE SAID, "I COME TO SEE HER."

The old woman said, "She's ailing."

"I don't believe she's ailing. I rode all the way out here through this damn snow to see her and I by god aim to see her."

He pushed the door back, the woman holding it fell back with it, and he stepped inside, not bothering to stomp the snow off his boots or knock it off his hat. The room was dim because of the poor winter light, but it was warm—almost too warm.

She was there, sitting in a rocker with a quilt over her and she was holding something, and he said, "Is that the kid?"

Her voice cracked with dryness. She still felt a little ill from it all, a little poorly, and the infant hadn't wanted to nurse, even though she'd been trying to get her to all morning.

"What you want, Dallas?" she said.

"I want to know is that him? Is that the kid?"

"Surely you can see it is a baby I'm holding," she said.

He stepped forward. She clutched the infant closer, keeping the quilt over it so he couldn't even see it.

He reached down to remove the edge of the quilt and then a small soft voice from in back of him said, "You leave her alone!"

He turned in time to see the boy, Frisco, pointing a small-bore rifle at him, the damn thing nearly as long as the boy was tall.

"Put that away!" Dallas ordered.

The boy shook his head.

"Ain't gone do it."

"Boy, I'm gone whip you bad, you keep pointing that goddamn thing at me."

"You leave him alone," Marybeth said.

"I'm gone whip his ass he don't quit pointing that gun at me."

"You get out!" the boy said.

The old woman joined in by screaming, calling him a "son of a bitch."

He said, "What the hell's wrong with you people!"

The boy said, "I'm gone shoot you in the guts."

Two quick steps and Dallas wrenched the gun from the boy's hands, then took his hat off and slapped him hard across the face, knocking him to the floor. The hat left red welts on the boy's cheek. The boy put his fingers to his face, tears leaking out his eyes. Dallas broke open the gun and extracted the shell and put it in his pocket, then tossed the gun aside and turned back to the girl.

"Now let me have a look at that goddamn kid!"

"Go on and look," she said defiantly. "I want you to look."

He pulled away the top of the quilt, the part covering the infant's head.

"Son a bitch!" he said when he saw. "I knew it."

"You happy now?"

"Son of a bitch," he said again. "I don't believe it. It's

his kid. You went and let that son bitch knock you up with his kid!"

"Yes!" she said.

"Son bitch."

Then for a moment there was just silence.

"I ought to shoot you," Dallas said.

"Go ahead."

The old woman screamed again and Dallas told her to shut her mouth and she did. Frisco scrambled for the gun, thinking he'd use it like a club, and hit Dallas across his legs with it, but again the cowboy stepped quickly, kicked the gun away, and warned: "You try one more thing, I'm gone beat you like a mule."

The girl wept openly, bitterly.

"You ain't got no affair with none of this," she sobbed. "Whyn't you go on and leave us all alone. Ain't you done enough already? You killed Nat and now you want to kill me. Well, just go ahead and kill us all if that's what you're intending, 'cause it don't matter to me. Kill this baby, too! Kill Nat's baby girl."

He stood there breathing hard through his nostrils. He had it in mind to do that very thing: to kill every last one of them.

"You're all just white trash," he said to the girl. "Just goddamn white trash, is all!"

The baby began to cry and she held it up close to her and tried to put her tit in its mouth, but it fussed and wouldn't take it and her milk leaked down onto its face and she cried even more.

He didn't know what to do. The old woman was crying, too. Out of frustration he upturned the table and the things that were on it: some old china dishes and cups they had brought with them from Arkansas; a jar with dried wildflowers in it—Nat's last gift to her he'd brought that late fall: "I found these just waiting for you, Marybeth," he'd said, giving them to her—a tin cup with coffee in it the boy had been drinking. All of it scattered across the puncheon floor like trash now.

He removed the pistol from its holster and cocked it and aimed it at her and said, "Yes, I killed him and I'll by god kill you, too, woman. You and this old hag and that boy yonder."

He could see it then, the fear in her eyes, and that is what he wanted to be there. The baby cried louder still. It squirmed in her hands and she felt completely incapable of caring for it. Dallas pulled the trigger and the sound of the pistol fire was like an explosion in the small room. The bullet took out a chunk from the wall above her head. The explosion seemed to stun them all into silence, except for the babe, who screamed even louder—though its cries were hardly more than the squalling of a kitten.

"Let that be a warning to you," he said. Then he said something strange, something none of them expected.

"You get rid of that and I'll take you in. You don't and I will kill you."

She shook her head.

"You got one day to think about it," he said. "You get rid of that and I'll come back here for you and you can go with me. These others can make their own way, only I don't want them around here no more."

And when no one said anything, he added, "I ain't fooling around. And if you think the law will protect you, you better start thinking otherwise, because he's on my list, too. Get rid of it, or else!"

It seemed like they didn't breathe until they saw him riding away.

Frisco said, "He's gone, the son of a bitch."

"Hesh, with that sort of talk," the old woman said. "You sound just like him when you talk like that."

"I don't care if I do."

"I care if you do. I don't want to hear no more cursing."

"He comes back, I'm gone shoot him in the guts."

"Oh, god!"

The girl didn't say anything.

The babe had finally clamped onto her breast and began suckling a little. Tears fell from her cheeks onto the tiny hands that had turned into fists, as though it knew already it was going to have to fight for every little thing in life.

The boy stood staring out the window, hoping that Dallas would come back, even though he had nothing to shoot him with.

The old woman closed her eyes against it all. *Why is life so rotten bad?*

20

JAKE AWOKE TO THE SMELL of frying bacon, coffee, and baking biscuits. He dressed quickly and went out into the kitchen, where the girls were already seated at the table and Clara was busy serving them their breakfast.

"Good morning, Mr. Horn," the girls said in unison. They had happy smiles on their faces and he felt more than a little embarrassed.

"You forgot to comb your hair, Mr. Horn," April said.

"Yes, you forgot to comb your hair," May said with a giggle.

He swept his fingers through his hair, trying to smooth down the wild parts.

"Mr. Horn slept over as our guest last night, girls," Clara said.

They looked at her with bright expectant eyes.

"Now, let's not bother him," Clara added. "Mr. Horn, are you hungry?"

He nodded and said, "I need to go check on my patients first."

"Mr. Horn stayed the night as our guest because he has two men he's caring for in the infirmary," Clara said. "They're very ill and he didn't want to leave them."

"Yes, Mama," they said.

"I'll be right back," Jake said.

"Call me if you need my help," Clara said.

Ellis Kansas was dead.

He lay on his back with his mouth slightly open, his eyes staring at the ceiling. Jake thumbed the man's eyelids closed. It felt the way it always felt when a patient died on him. Like a defeat. He took it personally.

He turned his attention to the scraggly young man.

"I'm pissing blood," Willy Silk said.

"I think you may have suffered a wound to one of your kidneys, but I don't think it was very deep."

"Hurts like a bastard."

"I'm sure it does."

"Am I gone live or not?"

"Probably," Jake said.

"How can you be sure?"

"If you were going to die, you'd have died by now."

"Like him?" Willy nodded toward the body of Ellis Kansas.

"Yes, like him."

"What was it killed him?"

"Somebody shot him through the neck."

"God*damn*."

"You'll need bed rest for a few days," Jake said.

"Why, if I ain't gone die?"

"Because you could get that wound infected and then you would die. Besides, I doubt you'll feel like walking very much for awhile."

Willy tried to sit up, but the pain was excruciating.

"I'm thirsty."

Jake brought him a glass of water and held his head while he drank it.

"Damn thing is, it's gone make me piss more, ain't it?"

"Best to keep fluids in you," Jake said.

"Huh?"

"Drink lots of water. I'll set the pitcher and the glass here by your bed."

"This a hospital?"

"Infirmary," Jake said.

"And you're the doc?"

"City marshal," Jake said.

"You arrest that bitch who stabbed me?"

"Not yet."

"What the hell you waiting for?"

"She claims you assaulted her."

"Hell I did. She stabbed me over that Chinese girl."

"Why would she do that?"

"Shit, you best go ask her."

"I intend to."

Willy grimaced and Jake said he'd check in on him later.

Jake went back out and sat down at the table and ate the breakfast Clara fixed him. The girls excused themselves to go out and play. Clara and Jake could hear them whispering to each other as they put their coats on in the mud room: "Mama's in love with the marshal." "I know it." "*Shhh, shhh,* they'll hear us." Clara looked at Jake and shook her head.

"They asked me if I was in love with you," Clara said with a smile. "I told them not to be silly. But they're right. I am."

Jake didn't say anything, but stood away from the table and went to the stove and took the pot of coffee and refilled his cup.

"You want some more?" he said.

"No," she said. "I'm fine."

"Ellis is dead," he said. "I didn't want to say anything

in front of the girls. I need to go get John and have him take care of it, then I need to go over to the saloon and question that girl who stabbed the other one."

Clara watched him as he stood drinking from the cup. He could tell that she wanted to talk about what the girls had asked, but he wanted to avoid the subject for the time being. Too many things were on his mind. He finished and set his cup down, then went and put his coat on and Clara stayed sitting at the table.

"I'll come back in awhile and check on the young man. He should be fine until I get back. Unless you want to offer him something to eat. Though I doubt he'll feel like eating."

She nodded.

"We'll talk about that other thing, too," he said. "Only not now."

She looked expectantly at him, then said, "Okay."

He went to Tall John's and told him about Ellis.

"That's a shame," John said. "He seemed like a pretty good fellow, all around."

"Yeah, I think he was, too."

"I'll try and get him in the ground today, if it ain't frozen. If it is, I might have to put him in Zimmerman's icehouse, where he keeps his meats."

"Whatever you have to do," Jake said, "as long as you get him out of Clara's house."

"I'll go and find Will Bird and we'll get him out."

Jake went out and crossed the street and went down to the Three Aces. It was early yet. The barman was washing glasses and looked up when Jake stepped inside.

"I need to talk to the girl from last night," Jake said. "The one involved in the knifing."

"Sweetwater Sue? She's in the back, third door on the right."

Jake went on back and knocked and waited.

"Go away" came a feminine voice from inside.

"City Marshal, we need to talk."

He heard movement in the room, a second voice, then the door opened and the woman stood there in a loose-fitting kimono. He could see the other girl beyond, there on the bed, sitting with her knees pulled up—the Chinese.

"The man you stabbed last night," Jake said. "He says you did it for no reason, except maybe jealousy."

She saw him looking past her, stepped out of the room into the hallway, and closed the door behind her.

"He tried to rape me."

"Open your robe," Jake said.

"Go to hell."

"Open your robe so I can see the marks on you."

"What marks?"

"A man who tries to rape a woman will leave marks, bruises of some sort. I don't see any on your neck or arms, so open your robe."

"Look, I didn't give him a chance to put his hands on me. He acted like he was a customer, then when we get back here to the room, he tells me he doesn't have any money and that I'm going to give it to him for free or else he's going to take it. I asked him to leave and he refused. So I said I was going and he tried to stop me and that's when I stuck him."

"You stuck him in the back," Jake said. "How'd that happen?"

"Listen, mister, I been around enough men to know when they're dangerous. I don't give them a chance. Who's going to blame me?"

"Go get dressed."

"Why?"

"Because I'm going to arrest you."

"For what?"

"For your own good."

She laughed harshly.

"You're just like all the others," she said. "What, you want a free poke? You'll let me go if I give you a freebie?"

"Get dressed," he said.

He saw then the anger in her, enough anger to put a knife into someone.

"You son of a bitch," she said.

"You got two minutes."

He waited until she came out again, the Chinese girl clinging to her, pleading with him not to take her.

"No, no," she cried. "She takes care of me. Please!"

Jake ignored her and led the whore by the elbow down the hall, through the main room, and outside.

"Why are you doing this? Don't I even get a trial?"

Jake prodded her on until they got to the jail.

"Empty your reticule on the desk," he said. She did as she was told and when he saw she had no knife or other weapon—like a derringer—he opened the cell door and waited until she entered, then locked it behind her.

"How long you going to keep me here?"

"Until I can figure out who's telling the truth."

"I don't see you locked that son of a bitch up."

"He's not in much condition to walk."

She was flushed with anger to the point of trembling.

"I hate you!" she said.

"I know it. I'll send someone around later with lunch."

She was still cursing him when he stepped outside again.

* * *

The air had a cold crispness to it. It stung the skin, but it felt good, too. Except for the muddy horse-trodden street, everything appeared white and pure, like a painting of a winter scene he'd seen in an art museum once.

He wondered when the cowboys would come.

21

❖

FRISCO DROVE THE WAGON. Marybeth and the infant rode on the seat beside him. The old woman sat in the back, wrapped in blankets. It was slow going through the snow-heavy road. The horse labored and they had to stop often to let it blow.

"It feels like we're the only ones in the whole world," Marybeth said, looking around at the endless white landscape. Not so much as a crow flew to break the empty feeling.

Frisco said, "I don't know why we're running."

" 'Cause we ain't stupid, is why," the old woman retorted.

He looked around. She was his ma, but he never forgave her for running off his pa. She had a severe visage. Her tight face seemed little more than thin skin stretched over bones with gray empty eyes. He never knew her as anything but old, even though she claimed to be only thirty some years of age. He remembered his pa as a stout dark-haired man with handsome good looks and happy ways. But he remembered, too, the arguing the two of them did, mostly at night. The old man wore his pants tucked inside his boots and kept his black hair combed down the center and wore a black handlebar moustache, which he waxed diligently. He liked clean shirts, freshly boiled, and kept them buttoned at the throat. Marybeth had told the boy once that their pa had a woman in town he went to see regular and he asked her how she knew such a thing and she said their ma had told her. He didn't want to believe it, but whenever he looked at the old woman, he thought he could understand why his pa might take up with someone of a less sour disposition.

Her voice reminded him of a dog's bark.

"Stupid is as stupid does," he said bitterly.

The old woman said, "I ought to slap the sass out your mouth."

"Go ahead," he said.

She simply glared at him. They both knew it had come a point it wouldn't do any good to whip him, that if there was a man to be relied on among them, it was him, even if he was only around twelve years old. He was lean as a hungry wolf and had wolf's eyes, amber and fierce, like he'd swallowed all the misery there was to swallow and couldn't spit it back up again. He was old beyond his years, she thought. The girl, less so for having taken up with that colored cowboy and getting herself a belly full of child. But what was there in this far-flung frontier but cowboys and a few bachelor ranchers old enough to be the girl's father, most of them. The rest of the local manhood, as far as she could determine, were no-account, dumb as oxen, stubborn as mules, dirty, thieves, and worse. Look what the girl taken up with before Nat Pickett. Colored as that boy was, he was twice as better than that damn Dallas Fry, who was meaner than a snake.

Men were all the same in her book—not to be trusted or counted on and not a one of them worth the air they breathed. She thought about Harry, how he run off on her for some red-haired harlot, then left her, too, and God only knows where he went after that. She hadn't heard of him in years and she didn't care to, either. She figured he was dead. It never cost her a night's sleep to think he was.

"We better get on," she said. "That old horse is liable to die he stands there long enough."

Frisco snapped the reins and the horse didn't move, then he snapped them again and yelled, "Haw on!" and the horse stepped off, but you could see pulling the wagon with the four of them in it was a strain.

It took the better part of a day for them to reach Sweet Sorrow.

The old woman said, "Pull in here."

She said, "I'll go and get the marshal."

The girl said, "Hurry, I'm cold, Mama."

Inside the jail she saw a fat old man leaning back in a chair half asleep and she slammed the door hard and he near fell out of his chair.

Gus Boone thought somebody fired a gun.

"Jeez Christ!' he said, scrambling up.

"Where's the marshal?" the old woman said. "We come to see the marshal."

"He ain't here."

"I can see that, you dolt. Where is he?"

Gus shrugged. She looked like something in one of his nightmares.

She saw the woman locked up in the jail cell. *Floozy, for sure.*

"Well," she said, "perhaps you could tell me where I can find him before we're all murdered."

"Murdered?" Gus said. "Who's going to murder you?"

"I ain't about to discuss my business with you."

Gus looked befuddled.

The door opened and Frisco and the girl came in. It made the small room crowded with all of them standing in there. Frisco looked at the calendar on the wall. It had a drawing of a woman in a big hat holding a can of coffee that said ARBUCKLE IS THE COWBOY'S COFFEE. Then he saw the rack of guns—shotguns and rifles, repeating Winchesters, and double-bore Whitneys. He could do some serious damage to that son of a bitch with one of those. His own single-bore was out in the wagon, its stock cracked, its barrel pitted. He planned on taking the dime he had saved and buying himself a bullet to replace the one Dallas had pocketed. A bullet *for* Dallas, only next time it wouldn't end up in his pocket but in his goddamn guts.

"It's too cold for me and little Sadie to wait out there, Mama," Marybeth said.

Gus saw the girl had a baby under the blanket wrapped around her. And when she took the blanket from around its tiny head as she stood over near the stove, he could see it wasn't any bigger than a five-pound sack of Arbuckle. He never saw a baby with so much dark hair.

The woman in the cell watched them as well. And when Frisco noticed her, it did something to him, the way she was dressed, the way she looked. He wondered if she was the woman his daddy had kept in town. She looked a lot like a woman his daddy might take to: She wore a fancy dress.

The baby began to cry.

It troubled Gus to no end that it did.

Frisco went over the cell and looked at the woman and she looked at him. Her cheeks were rouged and her lips were red and wet as licked candy.

"You the woman that stole my daddy?" he said.

"I might have been," Sue said. "You just never know, now, do you."

The old woman came and grabbed the boy by the shoulder and turned him around and said, "Shut that little flannel mouth of yours!" Then she looked at the floozy and said, "I reckon there is a good reason why they got you locked up. I hope they throw away the key!"

Gus said, "Now, ladies."

And when they both looked at him as though they wanted to bash his head in, he said, "I'll go find the marshal."

Jake had stopped at the hotel to look in on Tig. The boy was sitting on the side of his bed, smoking a cigarette and looking glum.

"How is it going, son?"

The boy looked at him and mumbled, " 'Bout the same, I reckon."

"You go see the dentist yet?"

Tig shook his head.

"You been taking that laudanum regular?"

Again, he shook his head.

"I've got a problem, son," Jake said.

The boy stood and went over to the window and the smoke curled up from his cigarette and butted up against the glass and curled over and hung there in the air.

"Those who did this to you and killed your friend Nat," Jake said. "Well, they're going to ride in here and try and do the same to me. I need to know how many exactly I'm going to be dealing with when they come."

The boy looked around for a moment.

"Five," he said.

"Five," Jake said, contemplating the number. Five was a lot.

"You any good with a gun?"

Tig stared at something out on the street for the longest time, then shook his head.

"No," he said. "I ain't no good with a gun."

"I'll be honest with you," Jake said. "I've got no one to back me up. I thought maybe, considering what they did to you, you might want to get even."

Tig swallowed hard. The light fell on his swollen face and he smoked the cigarette slowly, each time exhaling against the window glass, his eyes seeming to study the shape the smoke took.

"Dallas and them will kill you and whoever stands with you," he said through painful lips. "I got no fight in me. I got to get on."

"You run from this, you'll regret it."

"I don't run, I'll regret it."

He dropped the smoldering butt of the cigarette and crushed it with his boot heel.

"I was planning on leaving in the morning," he said.

Jake said, "I understand."

It looked like the boy wanted to say something else, but when he didn't, Jake turned and went out and went down the stairs and out through the lobby. He was aware now of everything around him—the desk clerk, an old fellow sitting in the lobby reading a newspaper, the slow tock of the Regulator clock above the desk. He had begun to prepare himself for the confrontation with the cowboys and moved with caution, his gaze sweeping and registering everything. His only advantage was he didn't figure they'd come in separately; they'd come as a crew—it only made sense that they would. He looked up and down both sides of the street, did not see their horses tied up anywhere. Snow stood in drifts up against the boardwalk and along the east walls of the buildings. The wind was sharp and cold.

Gus Boone met him halfway back to the jail.

"There's some people looking for you," he said. "A kid and a old woman and a young girl with a baby."

Now what? he wondered.

Tig stood watching from his window. He admired the grit of the lawman, but thought him foolish to try and face down Dallas and Perk and the others. *But it ain't my trouble no more,* he told himself. *I had my time and I lost and this is what they did to me.* He moved away from the window and looked at his face in the speckled mirror that hung on the wall above a scarred commode. It was like looking at a ghost, he thought. Something ugly and awful and it caused him to cry to think of what they'd done to him and how he'd never be a handsome carefree young cowboy again. He drew back his lips and it was painful, and looked at the gap in his teeth, then quickly closed his mouth again. As much as he tried not to, his tongue kept finding that empty space where his teeth had been.

He went over and took the bottle of laudanum and drank some of it and tossed himself down on the bed.

God*damn*, god*damn*, god*damn*.

Jake entered the jail and saw them standing there, gathered around the stove, Frisco glancing back toward the whore in the cell.

"What are you doing here? Is the baby sick?"

"He come threatening to kill us all," the old woman shrieked.

"Who did?"

"That damn Dallas Fry!" she said. "He come and said if Marybeth don't get rid of it"—she pointed toward the infant—"he'll kill us all."

"When did this happen?"

"This morning."

He saw the girl nodding in agreement.

"We got no place to stay, mister," Marybeth said.

"Go on over to the hotel and get a room and tell the clerk to send me the bill."

"What about Dallas? You gone arrest him, or what?"

"Don't worry," Jake said. "I'll handle it. Just go over to the hotel."

He waited until they shuffled out, one following the other, saw them crossing the street and shuffling through the snow, a sad line of humanity. His anger toward the cowboys just got worse.

He looked at the woman in the cell.

He felt just as caged.

22

WILLY SILK LAY WONDERING about the prospects of death, something he had never allowed to enter his mind until now, with the searing pain in his back just below his ribs where the woman had stuck him with the knife. The man said he would probably not die, but how did the man know if he wasn't a doctor? And why was he still pissing blood into a bucket? It didn't take a doctor to figure out things were bad.

A woman came in to ask if he wanted some breakfast. She was fairly plain to look at, but not unhandsome, he thought. He liked the sound of her voice.

"No," he said. "I ain't up to eating."

"Well," she said, "here is a small bell. If you get hungry or decide you need something, just ring it."

"Who are you?" he said.

"I own this house. It was previously owned by a physician, and this part used to be his infirmary. My name is Clara Fallon."

"Oh," he said. "Well, I sure don't think I could eat anything."

She said, "Okay," then started to turn.

"That fellow," he said. "One who was doctoring me, said he was a lawman. What's his story?"

She turned back, but kept her distance from the bed. There was something about this man that frightened her a little. He had an innocent enough face, but there was something cruel and hardened in his eyes.

"He saved your life," she said. "He cleaned your wound and stitched you up. Somebody else might have let you die, but he didn't. Now, let me ask you something."

"What's that?"

"What's your story?"

"Lady, you don't even want to know."

"Sure I do, this is my house and I'd like very much to know who I'm dealing with under my roof."

"No, you wouldn't," he said, his gaze more intimidating than before.

"Fine," she said and went out again and his eyes followed her, the sway of her firm hips beneath the long blue skirt, but he had no interest in her in that way. The stabbing seemed to have ruined him on any woman because he'd been thinking about nothing but how much he hated them, what troubles they'd led him to ever since he had heard his own mother and his uncle Reese whispering behind closed doors that time. It was his first sense of betrayal by a woman and since that time there had been dozens of others.

He rolled onto his side and lifted himself painfully up and set his feet on the floor. It took a great lot of effort, hard work, like bailing hay or some such, just to do that much. He sat breathing hard, his heart pounding in his chest. Then, when things subsided, he stood and, Jesus, it was the worst damn pain he'd ever had and he had a hard time standing straight up and had to bend slightly at the waist in order to withstand it.

He shuffled over to a set of tall windows that let in the winter morning's light. They went from ceiling to floor and had wine-colored drapes hanging from either side, which had been drawn back away to let in the light. He looked out and could see some of the town down the way, the buildings standing under a blanket of fresh snow. The wintry sight reminded him of his childhood, of better and happier times. He looked upon the town with deep regret that it wasn't his town, his boyhood home. But there was something about it all that seemed familiar to him. He thought and thought through the ache of pain and the fog of laudanum. What was it, exactly, that seemed so familiar?

Maybe it was something about the man, the lawman. Had he met him somewhere before? Maybe at some shooting match? In a saloon, maybe? The light of sunlight glancing off snow was of such brilliance that it caused him to seek out something dark to stare at—a roof line, a telegraph pole—anything to relieve the ache of glare. He remembered eating snow. It had no taste, just a cold sharp sensation. Those were the days before his uncle Reese came along and ruined everything.

He shook his head thinking, trying to remember where he'd seen the lawman before. It didn't seem to want to come to him. Maybe it was just his imagination. For how many men had he run into in his journey, in his carousing and shooting matches? Pimps and gamblers and men who would come up to him after the shows he'd performed in with Colonel Lily's Wild West Combination. Men who wanted to shake his hand and look at his pistol and get his autograph. Men who wanted to introduce their wives to him, wives that often stole what he considered admiring glances. Maybe it was one of those men, one whose wife came to his hotel later that same evening, and knocked on his door and he would let them in and watch as they took off their clothes, saying, "You are a handsome young boy, Willy Silk. My husband can't stop talking about you and I couldn't stop thinking about you." And he would watch them dress again after brief and almost violent sex and they would shyly, more often then not, say, "Of course you know I've never been here, it was all just a dream we shared, Willy, you *do* know that, don't you?" And he would nod his head in ascent, knowing that the next day he would be in another town performing in another show and there would be other wives of men who wanted to shake his hand. The scenario repeated itself so often that maybe it was, after all, just a dream, now that he thought about it.

But honestly, he could not remember any particular face of someone who looked like the lawman.

He grew tired of standing there, leaning over to one side to relieve the ache, and limped back to the bed and lay down again, feeling sick from the motion. Then some men came in the side door and went over to the bed where the dead man lay and wrapped him in a blanket, grunting as they lifted the dead man, and carried him back out the side door again. They'd glanced at him once as they were doing their work, but didn't say anything, then they were gone and the room was empty and he was relieved that they had taken the dead man because he couldn't stand to look at him.

And later the woman knocked on the door, then came in carrying a silver tray and on it was a china teapot with a rose pattern and a matching cup and she set it down next to his bed on a small carved wood stand and said, "I thought maybe you might like some tea. I know you're probably one who likes coffee, but tea is much better for you when you're sick."

Then she stood for a moment staring down at him. She reminded him of his ma a little, only not quite so old. She had a kind face, the sort of face you'd want your sister to have.

"Thanks," he said, for that is what he thought she was waiting for.

He could hear the laughter of children somewhere in the house.

"You're welcome," she said and turned and went out again.

Tea, he thought. He'd never in his life drank tea.

What is it about that lawman? he wondered.

In the hotel room Marybeth Joseph repeated to Jake the incident that had brought them into Sweet Sorrow and he listened with more than a mild interest to what she had to say about how Dallas Fry had come and threatened them and what he said about her getting rid of the baby and the rest of it. He could see she was frightened and worried and wondered how it had come that a girl so young had bought herself so much trouble.

The old woman sat on the bed, huddled in a blanket, and looked on with startled eyes. Frisco stood looking out the window down onto the snowy street, watching men on horses ride up and down, teamsters hawing their loads, some of the merchants now shoveling paths from their doorways, pushing the snow out into the street. He saw two men standing and talking, one of them smoking a black cigar, both of them in black coats and hats, and wished he had shot Dallas Fry when he had the chance, instead of giving him a warning. His cheek still burned with humiliation at having been slapped and having his rifle taken from him. Soon as he could, he'd go find a store and buy himself another bullet.

"You got to help us," Marybeth was saying.

"Don't worry," Jake said, "I think you'll be safe here."

"Will you go and arrest him and lock him up?"

"Yes." Jake knew the lie would give them each some measure of comfort.

"Good," the girl said. "My baby doesn't want to nurse too well."

"Do you want me to look at her?"

"Yes," the girl said and held the baby forth and Jake examined the child and saw that its color wasn't the best; its skin was the color of pearl, a sign that it was malnourished.

"Send Frisco to the general store and have him buy a jar of honey and put a tiny bit on your nipples when you try and nurse."

The girl offered him a quizzical look.

"For the sweetness," Jake said. "The babe will suckle better."

"Where's the general store?" Frisco said.

"Follow me out and I'll show you," Jake said.

Once out on the street again, Jake pointed out Otis Dollar's place and told the boy that whatever he needed at the store as long as they were in town, to tell Mr. Dollar to put it on Jake's tab.

"Yes sir."

"Oh, and maybe get yourself some stick candy."

"I ain't no kid," Frisco said.

"I know you're not, just thought maybe you might like some."

The boy stuck out his hand for Jake to shake and Jake shook it.

"I wouldn't want to put you to no trouble, Marshal."

"It's no trouble, son."

Then Jake watched as the kid went on down the sidewalk, stepping through the piles of snow that the wind had drifted up and he looked just like a small man on a mission with his fists jammed down deep inside his coat pockets and his rough old felt hat jammed down atop his head.

"You let me out of this cell, let me escape, and I'll let you have some free," Sue said to Gus Boone, who was spooning out coffee grounds floating in his cup.

"Free?" Gus said, looking up.

She stood holding the bars of her cell door, her face pressed against them, and he could see how blue her eyes were—blue as a summer morning sky.

"I couldn't do that," Gus said.

"I need to get out of here. I can't leave Narcissa be by herself."

"You mean the China girl?" he said.

"Yes. She can't be by herself, she don't know how to take care of herself. She depends on me."

"You know, I heard rumors about you two."

"Oh, I don't care nothing about rumors. Let folks say what they want to. It don't make no difference to me."

"It's unnatural, what I heard about you and that China girl," Gus said, sipping some of his coffee and tasting the grit of grounds caught in his teeth and using a fingernail to pry them out.

"You let me out of here and I'll prove to you there ain't nothing unnatural about me," Sue said.

"It's a tempting offer. I mean, just the thought of it, but the marshal would lock me up and throw away the key if I was to let you escape over something like that. You mind me asking, though, how much is it you'd charge me, say, once't you was set free legal and working again, and I was to want to buy your services?" Gus had never bought himself a whore; he preferred spending his money on whiskey, thinking that the effects would last longer than they would lying with a woman.

Sue looked at him with those cool morning blue eyes and said, "If you had all the money in the world, Gus Boone, it wouldn't be enough for me to lay with you, you hairy son of a bitch."

He sort of had to grin about that and went back to picking the stray coffee grounds out of his teeth with a fingernail.

"You sure got a mean mouth on you, gal. You want a cup of this coffee or something?"

Willy Silk downed the last of the laudanum and lay on the bed, waiting for the effect to overtake him. And when at last it did, he saw his mother there in the corner of the room standing by the tall windows.

"Ma?"

"Yes, Willy."

"Ma, I thought you was dead. Reese told me you'd died."

She smiled and said, "Do I look dead to you, Willy darling?"

She moved closer to his bed and it scared him because he was certain she was a ghost and he said, "No, Ma, don't come no closer."

She hovered over him and he felt a breath of cold fall upon him and he began to shiver.

"I'm dying, ain't I, Ma? That's why you're here. You come to take me with you . . ."

"Beware, child."

"Beware of what?"

Then she began to fade and he reached out his hand to touch her, but there wasn't anything there to touch. Just cold air.

The coldness got in him and he trembled. Snakes crawled along the floor toward his bed.

"No! No!" he cried.

Clara heard him calling and hurried to his room.

"What is it?" she said.

She found him huddled in the corner of the bed, curled up and whimpering like a child, went over to him, put her hand on his forehead, and felt how hot his skin was.

"No, Ma!"

She could see his glassy eyes staring up at her, full of fear.

"Easy," she said. She was nearly afraid to touch him.

She saw the sheets were stained with blood.

"I'll go and get Jake," she said.

His teeth chattered.

And when the man returned with her a short time later, Willy Silk remembered where it was he knew the man from.

It was that fellow he'd been paid to find and kill.

That one the rich man in Denver had paid him to track down.

"Put a bullet in that son of a bitch and you'll make me a most happy man, Mr. Silk."

Ain't them the exact words he said?

Then the fever took full hold of him and sent him

tumbling into a strange world—one in which he saw faces and heard voices of his uncle Reese and his ma and saw the bad things they were doing together, forcing him to watch, and horses were running wild through a cornfield. And there was a river across which he had to swim, only he didn't know how he was going to do it, since he was fearful of rivers and deep water. On the other side of the river he saw a man waving to him, yelling at him to come across, and he knew that the man was his pa.

And the wives of men whose names were lost to him appeared before him, lined up like rows of angels, dressed in long white robes, their hair in flames, and they became a choir of voices whose power seemed to lift him straight up toward the sun.

Then the face of Reese leaned in close, his fetid breath sour and stinking, and said, "Go on over, Willy. Go on over to the other side of that river yonder."

But when he tried to cross that troubled water, he sank, and the water closed over him, cold and heavy, and the last thing he saw was the face of the man on the other side, the one he was sure was his pa, only it was the face of the lawman.

"What is it?" Clara said when she saw the boy's eyes roll white.

"The fever is burning him up," Jake said. "Help me carry him outside."

And as Willy Silk trembled, they carried him outside, for he was hardly more than a wasted young man, and laid him in a snow drift.

"He will freeze to death," Clara said.

"No, he won't. It's the only way I know to bring the

fever down quickly before it ruins his mind and maybe takes his life."

And for a time it was touch-and-go as to whether Willy Silk would live or not.

23

❧❦

BOB PARKER WAS SITTING AT THE TABLE, waiting for his breakfast, when he smelled something burning. He had been reading an article in *Frank Leslie's Illustrated Newspaper* about the assassination and subsequent death months later of President Garfield. There was a drawing of the assassin shooting Garfield in a train station.

"Says here," Bob commented to his wife, who sat near the fireplace, knitting, "that his doctors submitted a bill for eighty-one thousand dollars to Congress, but they called them a bunch of quacks."

His wife arched her eyebrows as she brought him a plate of eggs and set it before him. It was still dark outside, the sun now yet risen. Bob read on, moving his lips over each sentence.

"Quacks," he repeated. "I guess so. That poor man suffered greatly, according to this. Sounds like they spent all their time torturing him. Eighty-one thousand dollars."

Then he smelled the thing burning and looked up and looked over to the stove, where his wife was now standing, thinking it the flue might be plugged but it looked all right and he said, "Do you smell that?"

"Smell what?"

"That?"

She sniffed and wrinkled her nose.

"What is it, do you think?"

"I don't know."

He rose from his chair and went over to the window and looked out.

"Oh hell," he said.

"What is it?"

"The bunkhouse is on fire!"

He grabbed his coat and hat and went out in a rush, leaving the front door standing open. His wife closed it behind him and continued to watch out the front window toward the bunkhouse. The dark sky was tingeing crimson along the horizon, like a seam of thin blood seeping up from the earth. The snow was ghostly blue and reflected the fire around the bunkhouse. Bright orange flames shot up from the roof of the burning building. She saw her husband high-stepping through the deep drifts that had piled up between the main house and the bunkhouse.

By the time he got there, he was out of breath. The odd thing was the hired men were simply standing there, watching the place burn.

"You boys!" he shouted. "Pitch in and get water out of the well!"

But they didn't move, not a single one of the five.

He started to run to the well himself to winch up buckets of water.

"Form a line!" he called, but they didn't bother to even so much as turn around.

It stopped him short when he realized they weren't pitching in.

"What the hell is wrong with you all?"

Dallas struck a match and cupped it in his hands as he lowered the end of his cigarette down to it and let it catch hold, then snapped out the match and dropped it in the snow. You couldn't tell whether it was smoke or just the cold air he was exhaling.

"You-all don't raise a hand, you're fired, every god-damn one of you!" Bob Parker yelled as he went over and lowered a bucket down into the well and heard it splash when it hit water, then winched it back up again and ran with it—spilling half of what was in it before he got to the bunkhouse—and pitched what there was left against the flames coming out now through one of the windows, the heat busting the glass. The flames licked out like the fire was trying to eat the very air. The water hit the fire and hissed but didn't seem to do a thing to stop its ravages. It made him about as mad as he ever had been to think those boys were just standing there like a bunch of mules, watching him and not lifting a hand to help out.

He threw the empty bucket to the ground and it stuck in the snow.

"I want to know just what the hell is going on here!" he said.

"Looks like your bunkhouse is burning, is what," Dallas said. Bob could see the flames reflected in his dark eyes, could see the fire's glow flaring out over all their faces as they stood there, their hands jammed down inside their pockets.

"Well, that's it, then. You boys are fired as of this minute. I won't have a bunch of useless sons of bitches around here."

"I guess we'll just collect our pay," Dallas said, "and move on."

"Pay! Hell, there's your damn pay," Bob said, pointing toward the burning building. "You fire-bugged the place on purpose. I'd like to know why."

"No," said Dallas. "We'll collect our pay before we move on."

He could see them standing there watching him. They were all dressed and set to go. He saw then their horses saddled and tied off to the corral rail. The boys had their saddlebags and soogins tied on. It was something they'd planned out.

"I'll be goddamned you get a single dime off me!"

His wife called to him from the house: "Bob! What's going on out there?"

Dallas's gaze flicked toward the house.

"You want us to burn it down with her in it?" he said.

They had him whipped every which way there was, he could see that. He had no firearms to defend himself or her, had come running out of the house thinking it was an accident. He hated it like sin they'd gotten over on him again. He should have fired them all soon as he suspected they'd had a hand in Nat Pickett's death and the brutal thing they'd done to Tig. These were mean, onerous men without a lick of conscience.

"I'll have to go into town to the bank," he said. "I don't keep that much cash on hand."

Dallas smoked his shuck and watched the fire burn and a few minutes hardly went by before part of the roof caved in and sent a shower of sparks skyward lightening up the now purple morning sky and Perk whooped and slapped his big hat against his thigh and put it back on his head again, saying, "Son of a bitch, would you look at her burn!"

"Let's go see what you got in the house," Dallas said.

"A few dollars at the most, is all."

"Let's go see."

The others started to follow, but Dallas told them to wait and he slid the Colts out of his holster from underneath his coat and said to Bob, "Lead the way."

They came inside the house. She saw them coming, Bob and Dallas behind him trudging through the snow and couldn't understand why they weren't trying to put out the fire. Then the door swung open and they came inside without even bothering to stomp the snow off their boots first and it fell off in clumps there on her expensive carpet.

"Why, whatever . . ." Then she saw Dallas holding the pistol and started to shriek, but he said, "Shut up or I'll shoot you in the mouth!" And when Bob started to protest such treatment of his wife, Dallas hit him hard across the side of his neck with the pistol barrel and the blow caused him to stumble and fall down on one knee, striking it hard against the floor.

"Go on, git up, you ain't hurt," Dallas ordered.

Bob struggled to his feet.

"Now let's go get the money."

Bob Parker led him into what looked like a study, a place with bookshelves and books on them and a big oak desk sitting in the middle of the room, and behind it a wood chair with cowhide covering the back and seat and some along the arms.

"Show me the safe," Dallas said.

"What safe? There ain't no safe."

"Goddamn but I'll hit you again you keep it up."

"Oh, Bob, just give him the money so's he can go on and leave us alone."

"Go sit in that chair," Dallas said to her. And when she did, he said, "Now quit fucking around here or you'll be sorry you did."

The safe was behind a horsehair divan in the corner. A little safe on wheels with gold lettering on the door: IN-GRAM'S SAFE CO. Bob knelt before it, his fingers trembling as he tried working the combination. He thought he had it but when he tried the handle it wouldn't open. Dallas stepped in close to him, stood over him and cocked the pistol and laid the muzzle against the back of his head.

"First I'll shoot you, then her. But before I shoot her, I'll let the boys take a turn with her then shoot her. That what you want?"

"Jesus Christ," Bob Parker blubbered. "I'm trying."

"Try again. You got one last chance."

The rancher steadied his hand and got the combination right and this time when he tried the handle the heavy door swung open. He kept a little two-shot derringer in it, right atop his money, thinking a time like this might some day come and what a grand surprise it would be for the son of a bitch who tried to rob him. But there it was and he had no will to grab it, no will, or no nerve either one.

Instead his fingers moved the little gun to the side and took the stack of money, which he knew rightly was just a little over fifteen hundred dollars—what he liked to think of as his rainy-day money.

"Here," he said, offering up the money.

Dallas looked at it, then stuck it down in his coat pocket with his free hand.

He didn't say anything for a time, just stood there breathing through his nose.

"Ah hell," he said and pulled the trigger.

Perk and the others heard the gunshot and started toward the house. Then they heard another just as they reached the front porch and Dallas came out through the door, closing it soundly behind him.

"What happened?" Perk said.

"Just a little misunderstanding, is all. He tried to shoot me with a little two-shot derringer" and he tossed it to Perk, who caught it, but when he broke it open, he could see there were two unspent shells still in it. Then he caught the look on Dallas's face and understood what the situation was.

"Let's ride," Dallas said.

"What about the money?"

"Son of a bitch had him a safe in there, but all he had in it was papers. I think he was telling the truth about it being in the bank."

"So it means we ride out busted as the day we rode in?" Taylor said.

"Well, unless you boys want to wait around and sleep in the snow."

They strode to their horses.

"What about that other thing?" Perk said.

"Yeah, we're gone take care of it. We're gone ride into town and get us a few drinks and maybe a little breakfast and then we're gone take care of it."

They mounted their horses, which were a bit rank from lack of being ridden very much over the weeks it took the men to dig the new well the boss had wanted, and Taylor's tried bucking him off and he cursed it and fought it to a standstill and said, "These goddamn nags are all rough" when it quit bucking.

Perk said, "You never was much with horses."

The bunkhouse was still in flames, but most of the rest of the roof had collapsed and there were just some of the walls standing now. And when they'd ridden off a mile or more, they looked back and could see the flames still rising and falling like something breathing and the sun was just edging its way over the horizon, shoving back the now gray sky, its rays spreading out over the snow causing it to sparkle.

"Maybe we should have burnt the whole place," Perk said as he rode alongside Dallas with the others trailing behind riding in single file because it was easier work riding through the deep snow to ride one behind the other.

"Maybe," Dallas said.

"What we gone do after we take care of that lawman?" Perk said.

"I don't know about you, but I'm about headed out of this country myself."

"I don't blame you after what you did back there."

Dallas looked at him hard.

"Whatever went on back there, we're all in it together, don't you forget that."

"I know it. You know me, Dallas, I'm loyal to a fault, but what about them?"

Dallas didn't bother looking over his shoulder at Taylor and the others.

"It's every man for himself once we clear this country, I reckon."

"I was thinking."

"'Bout what?"

"Maybe we ought to rob the bank."

"My, ain't you gone and got big ideas."

"I know you shot them two back there."

"So what if I did?"

"Like you said, we're already in it together. Might just as well go on and make us some money long as the law will be looking for us anyway."

Dallas turned halfway around in his saddle and looked

back at the others now, riding with their heads down to protect their faces from the cold. A chill wind had begun to stir.

"They're as dumb as rocks," he said.

"Don't take no brains to rob banks, I reckon."

"All I want to do right now is take care of that goddamn son bitch lawman."

"I know it, but then afterward we could rob the bank. Might just as damn well. We kill that lawman, who's gone stop us from taking the bank?"

"Make me a shuck, I'm all out of makings."

Perk removed his gloves and tucked them down inside his coat pocket then reached up inside and took out his makings from where he kept them in the pocket of his shirt and set about making a shuck and when he finished he handed it over to Dallas.

"Here," he said.

Dallas took it and struck a matchhead off the horn of his saddle and cupped it in his hands and lowered his cigarette to it until it caught.

"Hell, maybe we ought to," he said.

"Then ride south, the bunch of us, we could rob all the damn banks from here to Texas I imagine, have us enough money time we got down there we could live like barons."

The idea was beginning to take root, Perk could see that when Dallas drew on the shuck and the way his eyes looked.

"Otherwise, we'll end up doing the same old thing—if we ain't caught and hanged—well-digging and fence-riding and cutting the nuts off steers," Perk added.

They rode along like that, thinking about it, the others in a single line behind them, cold and uncertain of their futures. Dallas had pretty much ruined them in this part of the country with burning down the bunkhouse and all the rest.

But they were men of a solitary nature and futures never did hold that much truck with any one of them. There was always another place to drift, always another job to do sooner or later. And if worse came to worst, they were sure old Dallas would come up with a plan.

Taylor said to Lon, "Look it how purty the sky's becoming."

Lon looked up and so did Harvey.

"This is real sky country, ain't it?" Lon said.

Harvey dropped his head back down; the wind hurt his face.

24

JAKE WAS STILL AT CLARA'S when the evening came.
Willy Silk's fever had finally broken and he had sunk
into a deep sleep. Jake said, "I ought to stay close, in case
the fever comes back."

Clara fixed them supper and the girls set the table.

"Why not light some candles," she said to the girls.
"Instead of lamps, let's eat by candlelight."

Of course it thrilled them to do so and they took turns
lighting the candles with Jake's help. And when he finished helping them, he went into the kitchen and said, "Is
there anything I can help you with out here?"

She was standing at the stove, cooking something in
one of the pots, stirring it with a wooden spoon, when he
came up behind her and asked her the question.

"You could put your arms around me," she said.

"Oh."

"Yes, like that," she said when he gently put his arms
around her waist. She leaned her head back slightly to
rest on his shoulder.

"What will we do about our troubles?" she said.

"Let's not talk about it tonight. Besides, it isn't our
troubles, but mine."

"No, you're wrong, Jake."

"Clara. I want you to do me a favor."

"Yes, of course, anything."

"If things go bad for me, I want you to send this to my mother." He handed her an envelope already addressed.

"Yes," she said, her voice reluctant to accept that things might well go bad for him. "Is there anything else you'd want me to do?"

"I've saved a little money," he said. "It's back in my hotel room with the rest of my things. Use it to pay John with and a burial plot. Whatever is left over, give to the girls."

"Oh, Jake . . . please don't . . ."

"It's necessary. You're the only one I can count on, Clara."

Clara felt her eyes fill up with tears.

"Would you slice the bread?"

"Sure," he said and got the cutting board down and the bread knife and began slicing the freshly baked loaf of bread she'd recently pulled out of the oven and set to cool by the frosty window.

At the table Jake sat across from Clara, April sat to her left, and May chose to sit next to Jake. The girls swung their legs as they ate and for dessert Clara served raisin pudding still warm with a nice covering of maple syrup she'd bought at Otis Dollar's mercantile earlier that week.

They ate mostly in silence, neither Clara nor Jake having much of an appetite. And later the girls helped Clara clear the table and wash the dishes while Jake sat alone in a highback rocker upholstered in red damask where he could watch the flames in the fireplace.

He looked around at the large rooms, the nice furniture—all left over from the estate of the late Doc Willis and sold with the house. There were large oil paintings on the walls in gilt frames: a young boy in a blue shirt and trousers and white stockings, a scene of a sweeping canyon with a crashing waterfall, a hunting dog set on point. *This is more house than your average person needs*, he thought. *The houses of the rich almost always are.*

He grew drowsy waiting there by the fire, waiting for Clara and the girls to finish in the kitchen. He could hear them back there, the girls chattering away, Clara patiently answering whatever questions they had to ask.

His eyes closed and he allowed himself to relax. It felt like every muscle in his body was knotted up, the cold weather had troubled the old bullet wounds he suffered, had caused some of them to throb and ache, especially down low on the right side, where one of the bullets had shattered a rib.

It seemed like another lifetime ago that the men had shot him and left him for dead. It was like Sam Toe, the liveryman, said, "It's following you, ain't it?", meaning death. It did seem to hunt him like some old bird hound hunting game in the brush.

He must have slept, but only for a minute, it felt like. When he opened his eyes, the girls were quietly reading books there on the floor and Clara was sitting opposite him in one of the French provincial chairs with its white arms and legs and blue tapestry seat, watching him. She held a small glass of sherry.

"Oh," he said. "I must have dozed off."

"You need to rest, Jake."

"Yes, probably so." He smiled knowingly and she smiled, too, for last night they hadn't done very much actual sleeping and he'd arisen early.

He waited until she put the girls to bed.

"You are planning to stay the night, aren't you?" she said. "I'd really like it if you were."

"Nothing would please me more, Clara, but I think I should probably go."

He saw the look of disappointment on her face.

"It's just that I think I need to prepare myself for what's coming and I can't do that here. When I'm here, I can only think of you and the girls." He didn't want to tell her that the real reason was that he didn't want to draw trouble to her door. He wanted to draw it as far away from her as possible.

When she didn't come and put her arms around him, he went to the entryway where he'd hung his hat and coat and took them down and put them on. She followed him at a distance and said, "I really wish you'd stay with me, Jake. I like having you in my bed."

"I like it, too, Clara. But not this time, okay?"

He stepped toward her and she stood stiffly as he kissed her lightly. He could tell that she was reluctantly accepting his feelings.

"Okay then," he said and opened the door and stepped out and closed it behind him quickly and quietly.

It had quit snowing, but now with night and the greater cold, the snow had a crust to it and it broke and crunched under his boots as he walked off toward town. A full moon stood in the black sky almost as white as the snow. The entire grasslands seemed to glow and when his gaze swept across them it seemed that the world was empty, a place where if you walked out far enough you'd simply fall off the edge and disappear. If only it were that simple.

He thought he could stand a drink, but then reason told him the last thing he needed was to have a head full of whiskey if those cowboys came. So instead he went straight way to his hotel room and shucked off his coat and took his Scofield pistols and laid them on the bed next to him as he lie there waiting for them to come. It was about all he could think to do: Wait for them to come.

25

❧❦❧

TIG WAS STANDING AT THE BAR, down at the end by himself. He didn't want any company and nobody seemed
to want his company, either. Word spread fast in this
place when there was trouble, when someone was having
trouble with someone else. And by now most everybody
knew the troubles Tig had with the other cowboys out to
the Double Bar and it was the sort of trouble none of
them wanted any part in. Dallas Fry was a fellow you
didn't want to get on your bad side.

The kid stood sipping the whiskey and beer back al-
ternately through his still sore mouth. The bartender had
served him, taken his two bits, and moved back down to
the other end, where most of the rest of them stood, those
who weren't sitting at tables gambling or in the back with
whores.

He could hear men conversing about the cold weather
and cattle and how rank horses would get over the winter
if you didn't ride them regular. He could hear their jokes
and comments about women.

Him and Nat used to come in and drink and laugh and
tell jokes and talk about women, too, until Nat took up
with that Marybeth Joseph. That's when it all started—

the trouble. Up till then, things were good. He sipped his beer and felt the bitterness rising in him again. As hard as he tried to fight it down, it kept coming back on him. Seemed like it had crawled down in him and burrowed somewhere and he couldn't get it to leave.

The bartender came over and said, "You want something?"

Tig looked up and said, "No, why?"

"You was talking, saying something, I couldn't understand from down there. I thought maybe you was wanting another beer or something."

Tig looked at his beer glass. It was half-empty, the shot glass still had some in it, too.

"No, I don't need no more—not yet anyways."

The bartender nodded and slapped the bar rag over his shoulder, moved back down to the other end, and started talking with the men down there. Tig could see some of them looking his way.

Then one of the whores came up next to him on the opposite side and it startled him a bit to realize she was standing there. She was the one he knew they called the China Doll, small and dark with those mysterious eyes, and she said, "You buy me drink?"

Tig looked at her a long time, then said in a slurred way because of his missing teeth, "You want me to buy you a drink?"

She nodded her head.

"Yes. You buy me drink, okay. Maybe we have a good time you like."

He pointed toward the bartender, who seemed to know already what was needed, and poured out a shot glass from one of the bottles lining the backbar and brought it down and set it in front of them.

"That's four bits," he said.

"Four bits? Hell, that's what I paid for a whiskey and a beer."

"The company's not exactly free, cowboy."

Tig looked at the China Girl, then dug a silver dollar out of his jeans and dropped it on the oak.

The girl took the glass and held it up for him to touch with his beer glass and he did and she sipped some of the whiskey and said, "You want to have good time with me?"

"I don't think so," he said. Normally he would have been all over the idea, but with his mouth sore and his feelings way down low, he didn't think he wanted to socialize with the whore.

Her face changed to a pout he couldn't be sure was sincere or not. He didn't know all that much about women, what they were really like. His experience had been limited to a few prostitutes and so he couldn't read them like he could horses. He felt foolish and uncertain with the way she was acting.

"Please," she said.

He looked at her again.

"I got to get on," he said.

"Where you go?"

"About as far away from this place as I can find."

He saw her looking at his face, the hole in his mouth where his teeth had been. He held his hand up to his face in an attempt to hide it from her. She swallowed the last of the whiskey.

"You buy me another drink?"

"Ma'am, I got about enough money to get me maybe as far as Bismarck and after that I'll have to pick up some work till I can make it down to Texas or somewheres."

"I have idea," she said.

"Oh, and what would that be?"

"You come." She took hold of his sleeve and tugged at

him and he reluctantly set his beer glass down and followed her toward the back and he could see some of the other men watching them, but he didn't care nothing about it.

They went down the hall he knew from before, when him and Nat would come in town together. He knew it was where the whores did their business because he and Nat had come back there with them when they had money in their pockets to buy a whore.

She led him into one of the rooms and closed the door behind her.

"Like I said, I ain't gone spend what little I have for a woman," he said. He was trying his best to be courteous about it.

"I give it to you free," she said.

"Free? Why would you do that?"

"I don't speak English so well," she said.

"Hell, that's okay. You speak it well enough."

"I have friend in jail. I need get her out."

Tig shook his head.

"I don't see what that's got to do with me."

"You help me get her out, I give it to you free."

"Get her out. You mean, go her bail?"

"Help me get her out," she repeated. "We trade."

"You mean, bust her out of jail?"

The China Doll nodded and pointed at the revolver resting on Tig's hip in the leather holster.

"Well, shit, I ain't no lawbreaker," he said. "I can't afford no more trouble than I got already. Can you understand that?"

She took his hand and placed it down the top of her dress and her breasts were warm and soft and, to tell the truth, he couldn't hardly stand touching her like that without wanting to keep on touching her. In spite of how he'd been feeling, he was feeling a little something other than pain and misery, now that he was touching her. He'd felt so alone since Nat's death and since the torture Dallas and them laid on him, felt so alone he wanted mostly just to die. The warmth of her flesh against his hand nearly brought him to tears.

"You like me?" she said

"Yes," he said, swallowing hard. "I like you."

"You help me?"

"She over there alone in the jail, do you think?"

The China Girl shrugged.

"Maybe she alone."

"This first, then that?"

"Yes. I give it to you, then you help me."

She seemed to yield under his touch and slid the top of her dress completely down so that he could see her, so that his hands could touch her where they wanted to. His heart raced rapidly. She was beautiful and small and delicate as a prairie flower.

"I won't kill nobody for this," he said as she pulled him over to the bed.

"No. You just help me get her free, okay."

"Okay," he said.

Then he waited while she undressed herself, then began to undress him.

"I do everything for you," she said.

"Yes. You do everything for me," he said.

And for a time nothing seemed to matter anymore.

Tig lay there feeling the ministrations of her body, her hands, her mouth. Even when she kissed him, her kiss was so tender that it felt more like a butterfly's wings touching his bruised mouth than a kiss. Her sex seemed to heal all the broken places inside him and it made him start to feel human and normal again.

He didn't know how long it went on. But finally they were finished with the first half of their bargain and she rose and dressed again and he watched her bone-smooth body disappearing into the dress and stockings. Tig watched as she pinned her thick long black hair up atop her head and took a rough old hat hanging on a peg and settled it down on her hair, tucking it up under.

"You help me now," the China Doll said, and he rose and dressed without taking his eyes from her.

"I'd never disappoint you," Tig said, feeling like maybe he could even be a little in love with her, knowing he'd do anything for her, even kill somebody if it came down to that. What did anything matter if you didn't feel right?

He put on his own hat and coat and she put on her coat, an overly large wool mackinaw and she looked nearly like a boy under that rough hat, except for the most delicate bones in her face.

"Can I kiss you again before we go out in that cold, ma'am?"

"Yes, you kiss me if you like."

And she stood on tip toes for him to kiss her and when he had she said, "We go now, okay."

She led him out the back way, instead of them going out through the bar again. He figured he knew why: They were gone bust somebody from jail and it wouldn't be wise to have half the men in town see them going to do it together.

They stepped out into the night and the cold air nearly took their breath away, even while their bodies were still warm and damp from their spent passion. The cold especially hurt his mouth and he flinched until he got used to it and they crossed over the street, trudging through the crusted snow, and went down toward the jail.

It was a lonely sound, them walking through the

crusty snow, and when they arrived at the jail they saw it was dark inside. Tig tried the door, found it to be locked.

"I'm gone have to bust a window to unlock it," he said.

The China Doll didn't say anything. He could see she was shivering.

"Well, here goes." He took the butt of his revolver and tapped it against the pane of glass in the door, then reached in and slid back the bolt from the inside and swung the door open. They stepped in.

There was enough moonlight to barely see by and Tig banged his knee on the edge of a desk and it hurt almost as bad as his mouth.

"Who's there?" a woman's voice said.

"Sue, Sue!" the China Doll said.

"That you, Narcissa?"

"Yes."

"Oh, honey," she said. "Come here."

"Where they keep the keys?" Tig asked.

"Who's that with you, Narcissa?"

"He help get you out," the China Doll said. "He very nice."

"Keeps 'em in the desk drawer—top-right-hand side," Sue said.

Tig pulled open the door and found a key and went to the cell and unlocked it and the other woman rushed out and threw her arms around the China Doll and Tig didn't know quite what to do at the sight of it because it looked like they were more than just good friends when the woman kissed the China Doll on the mouth for what seemed like a long time. He stood there somewhat dumbly, waiting for somebody to suggest something, and when they went on kissing and hugging, he said, "Might be best if we was to just go on and get out of here."

The woman turned to him and said, "So you're Narcissa's friend."

"Yes ma'am, I reckon I am."

"How nice," she said, moving against him.

"Lord," he said when she put her arms around him and drew him close and began nibbling on his ear. "Lord."

Then he felt it—the hardness of something pressing into his belly—and looked down and saw she had his pistol pulled out of its holster and shoved up against him and heard her cock it back and it sounded like metal levers being shifted.

"Get on in there, sweet thing," she said.

He stepped back and she prodded him inside the jail cell like you might nudge a cow to go into a holding pen, then she closed the door and the China Doll locked it with the key.

"Sorry," the China Doll said. Her apology seemed sincere.

"Hell, not as sorry as me," Tig said.

He watched them go out together and close the door with the busted window pane behind them, then they were gone and he was alone.

He stood there feeling helpless, but worse than that, feeling foolish for having allowed himself to believe even for a minute that he and the China Doll had something going together—that she liked him somehow, when all she really wanted was to use him to bust her girlfriend out of the jail. He wondered if it had all been worth it.

He went and sat on the cot and drew the blanket that was there up around his shoulders. It had the woman's perfumed scent on it. It was the same scent as was on the China Doll and it caused him to feel even sorrier still.

"Hell," he said. "Hell . . ."

Later Gus came in rubbing his hands and not bothering to light a lamp, drunk and singing something low under his breath.

Then Gus said, "Sue, I decided to take you up on that offer." Tig replied, "Let me out of this damn cage."

Gus went back there, peered in, and said, "You ain't Sue."

Tig said, "You're damn right I ain't."

Gus was confused.

"How the hell!"

"Let me out," Tig demanded.

Gus found the key tossed in the corner and unlocked the door and Tig went out in a hurry and Gus stood there, still trying to figure out how things got so switched around. Nothing made sense anymore. *I better just stop drinking and get right and go on home to my old woman and see will she take me in or will she won't.* Then he lay down on the bunk and fell asleep.

26

THEY REINED IN at the Three Aces and dismounted stiffly. The cold had climbed down into their clothes and skin and settled into their bones and they tied off with stiff fingers and stepped up onto the walk, snow clinging to them like they were fence posts, and went in through the double doors. There were already puddles on the floor from others who'd come and gone that morning.

Presently there was just the barkeep leaning against the oak, reading a *Police Gazette*, sipping coffee. He had a gut and black handlebar moustaches and looked up with a tired expression when they came in.

"You boys sure are around early enough," the barkeep said.

"We could stand some hot grub," Dallas said, pulling off his gloves. Lon and Harvey and Taylor all drifted toward the big potbelly in the corner of the room. They rubbed their palms together and held them forth toward the hot metal. Perk stood alongside Dallas at the bar and said, "I'll take a whiskey to get started."

The barkeep pulled a bottle down and poured a shot into a glass and looked at Dallas and said, "You want a shot, too?"

"Hell, this is a bar, right?"

"You got any grub in the back—maybe some leftover luncheon meat from yesterday?" Perk said.

"Ain't got nothing left over, waiting for the butcher to come around with something," the barkeep said. "Try the Fat Duck Café up the street. That's where you'll find grub."

The boys by the stove looked around when they heard Perk and Dallas ordering whiskey and Taylor came over to the bar and said, "I'll have one of those, too," so the barkeep poured him out one and said to Perk and Dallas, "You all want another?" Perk pushed his glass toward the bottle and said, "Bears shit in the woods?" and the barkeep poured him another and poured Dallas one as well. "How about you boys?" the barkeep said, looking at Lon and Harvey, who were still standing in front of the stove.

"No," Lon said, "my stomach's a little sour this morning."

Harvey didn't say anything. He wasn't much of a talker.

"You seen the marshal around this morning?" Dallas said.

The barkeep shook his head. "No, just some old boys come in and had themselves a cye-opener."

"He keep a place around here?"

"Hotel, far as I know."

"You know which room?"

The barkeep shook his head and Taylor pushed his empty glass toward the bottle and said, "Pour me another." The barkeep did and he and Perk and Dallas took their time with the second round because whiskey was dear to a man with near-empty pockets.

"You all drink up," Dallas said, tossing back his, then took his gloves and pulled them back on again and

slapped his palms together. "Let's go get some grub."
Perk and Taylor threw back their drinks and followed
Dallas back out again, along with Lon and Harvey
falling in behind.

The sun was risen high enough now that it fractured
off the crystalline snow the wind had kicked up and it
caused them to duck their heads low as they walked up
the street to the café. They entered and there were but a
few customers still there—most having eaten already and
gone—the early risers and those who could afford to pay
for a meal instead of eating something at home.

"Let's sit by that window, so we can keep an eye on the
street," Dallas said. There was only one table directly in
front of the window and it was occupied by an old man
dipping slices of bread in his coffee and thinking about
something in his long ago past because he didn't seem to
pay any attention to them when they approached his table.

"Why don't you move to another table," Dallas said.

The old man looked up at them with eyes gray as
flannel.

"To hell you say."

"Go on, dad."

He looked at all five of them, then slowly stood and
took his plate and cup and wandered off to another table
farther back because when you're in the shape he was in,
you didn't pitch into a bunch of young hands looking for
a fight. He had had so many fights in his lifetime he
couldn't remember them all. But what he did remember
was how much getting into a fight hurt and how nothing
good ever came out of a fight whether you won or lost,
except maybe your reputation if you won.

Dallas sat down first, then Perk took up the seat next to
him. Then Lon, Harvey, and Taylor all settled into chairs.

"You figured it out yet?" Lon said. "What we're gone do and how and when?"

Dallas looked at him like he couldn't believe the third man down on the string would ask such a question.

The waitress came with a tray of coffee cups and a pot and set them down and they all watched her while she did and she felt her skin burning from the way they were staring at her. She knew Dallas and that ugly Perk by reputation, but the others she only knew slightly from seeing them in town on occasion. They wore rough clothes and old stained hats and long kerchiefs around their necks and heavy coats. She didn't like the way they stared at her, but there wasn't anything she could do about it.

"What can I get you gents to eat?" she said.

They ordered eggs and hash, biscuits and honey, and she walked back to the kitchen knowing they were still watching her and it wouldn't take any sort of genius to figure out what they were thinking.

"We're gone get some grub in us and drink a little and if that son of a bitch happens to come walking in while we're doing it, we'll settle his hash here and now," Dallas said, answering Lon's question.

"And if he don't come in?" Taylor said, undoing the buttons of his coat.

"If he don't, we'll go pay him a visit over to the hotel where that barkeep said he stays."

"Then what? After we take care of this business?"

Dallas leaned in close to speak to them and they all leaned in close to listen.

"Perk and me has come up with a plan."

"What's that?" Taylor said. He had drops of coffee dew in his moustaches.

"We're gone rob that bank they got here, the one that the boss says he keeps all his money in."

He waited to see their reaction. None of them said anything. He looked at Perk, who said, "You boys ain't weak sisters, are you?"

Taylor straightened and said, "No, we sure as hell ain't, are you?"

Perk looked at him with those funny eyes and Taylor chose one to stare back at.

"You-all keep a watch on the street, in case you see that lawman," Dallas said. He could see they were thinking it over, about robbing the bank. He didn't know if any one of them, except Perk maybe, had ever broken the law or not. Well, they'd soon enough find out.

"Make me a shuck, Perk."

Perk took out his makings and rolled a cigarette and handed it to Dallas, then rolled himself one while they waited for their grub to arrive. And when it did, they set to eating like a pack of dogs because their feelings were running high from burning down the boss's bunkhouse and quitting on him and all the uncertainty about their futures and whatever it was they were set to do they were set to do it in a hurry, eating included. *Winter is a tough time to quit a job unless you got another waiting for you,* Harvey, the silent one, thought as he ate his eggs and hash. *I don't know about robbing no damn bank.* But he didn't say anything. He guessed whatever the others were up for doing, he'd go along with because he didn't know what else there was to do. *Was it spring or summer when a man might catch on with another cow outfit, I might just tell 'em all to go to hell and get on my own way, but things are tight and a man has to stick with his own kind in times of trouble.*

They ate, scraping their forks off their plates and watching the street in between, then sopping up the leavings with warm biscuits covered in honey. Taylor licked his fingers when he finished what was on his plate and looked around like maybe something else was coming, then rubbed the tip of his nose with the back of his wrist.

The waitress came over and set their bill on the table and nobody reached for it until finally Dallas picked it up and said, "This one's on me, boys."

He'd taken the trouble to peel off a few dollars from what he'd stolen back at Bob Parker's place and put it in a separate pocket on the trip to town without any of them seeing and he reached in and took out the spare money now and held up the bill, looking at it, then laid several dollars there on the table.

Perk said, "You gone leave that gal a tip?"

Dallas looked at him.

"Tip for what, she'd just doing her job, is all."

Lon dug around in his pocket and found a liberty-head dime and set it beside his plate and said, "I'll leave her a little something."

Then they sipped what was left in their coffee cups and set them down again and buttoned their coats and Dallas said, "Well, let's go get this done."

Gus Boone had seen them when they came out of the saloon and crossed the street to go into the café. He'd been talking to Will Bird in front of the barbershop. Will was telling him how he helped Tall John dig a grave and bury Ellis Kansas the day before.

"Clear into the evening we dug," Will was saying. "We was still digging when it got dark, that damn ground hard as iron, so's we had to use picks and I broke the handle on mine and had to go get another and finally we got it dug and here it is dark and beyond and my hands about so sore I can't hardly unbutton my fly to take a leak—"

"Lord, look what the cat's gone and dragged in," Gus said when he saw the boys crossing the street to the café.

Will looked around and saw them, too, and said, "You gone go tell the marshal?"

"Damn right. They dint just come in to eat, not on a Monday morning when they should be working. You better go let others know there's gone be a fight this morning and to keep the women and kids off the streets."

Will stood there, squinting against the sun and blowing snow. Seemed an awful day for a fight, cold and wintry as it was. But then blood only knew blood and death didn't know when to quit and all he could think was he didn't want to dig any more graves soon, his hands sore as they were and maybe he ought to go and get the waitress and make sure she was safe. He was pretty sure by now he was in love for the first time and he'd hate for anything to happen that would get in the way of all that. Should he go and make sure she was safe then tell the others, or tell the others then find Fannie? He was a little bit confused about what he should do exactly, and just stood there watching as those Double Bar boys came marching out of the café again.

Finally he turned and went up the street in a hurry and began telling everyone he encountered about what was happening and they should get off the streets unless they wanted to get shot, his voice becoming more high-pitched as he went.

* * *

Clara sat in stony silence as the girls watched her without speaking. Then she heard the tiny bell ringing from the other room and rose and went back to the infirmary.

"Wonder if you could tell me what you did with my clothes," Willy said.

"I cleaned them and they are hanging in the closet."

He looked around, then said, "Ma'am, I need to thank you for your kindness."

"You're welcome," she said.

"I had me some bad nightmares," Willy said. "Some things come to me and made me realize some things."

She didn't know what he was talking about and he didn't seem to want to explain it any further than that. She could only think about Jake as it was, and not about what this boy's problems were or were not.

"I just mean to say, I probably didn't show any gratitude toward you for helping me out here is all," Willy said. "I got to get on now, though."

"I don't believe you should try and go very far just yet," she said. "Jake . . ."

"You mean that feller who took care of me?"

"He saved your life," she said.

"I don't know why the hell he did. It sure ain't worth saving, far as I can see."

"It's his nature," she said, "even if it isn't yours."

He looked at her quizzically, then said, "Ma'am, you don't mind, I'd just like to get dressed now."

She nodded and turned and went out of the room and back into the parlor, where the girls still sat stiffly upon the divan.

"Mama," they said when she entered.

"Come here to me," she said.

They came to her and she wrapped her arms around

them and drew them close and wept and in a little while they heard the back door open and then close again and they could see through the window the man limping through the snow.

27

❖

JAKE ANSWERED THE KNOCK. He half-expected it.

Gus stood there, his nose red, dripping snot.

"They're here," he said.

"Where are they?"

"Over to the café."

"Okay, thanks."

"What you gone do, Marshal?"

"I don't know."

"You still got time to get the hell out. I could go and get you a horse and tie it up around back. Wouldn't nobody blame you."

"No."

"You know the day old Toussaint Trueblood found you and brought you here, you were all shot to pieces. You remember what it was like? You sure you want to go through all that again, only this time worse?"

"I'm not sure of anything, Gus. You want to walk over to the café with me and confront those men?"

Gus licked his lips.

"You know if I could shoot worth a damn, I'd be right there with you, don't you?"

"I know you would. Go on, Gus, get off the streets before things get started."

"Jesus, Marshal, you don't know how bad I feel about all this."

"It's okay."

Gus continued to stand there until Jake said again, "Go on, Gus. Things will work out the way they're meant to."

Gus turned and hurried off down the hall and Jake saw him turn and go down the stairs, then he closed the door and went to the closet and opened it and saw the new suit hanging there—the one he'd bought a month before, before all the trouble began with the Double Bar boys. He wasn't sure at the time why he bought it, other than his past dictated that a man should always have at least one good suit of clothes for special occasions. He used to have a wardrobe full of good suits in his former life. So he ordered it from Otis, who took his measurements and a down payment and said, "I'll send the order off today and the suit should be here in two weeks."

And when the suit arrived Otis said, "Aren't you going to try it on to make sure it fits?" Jake said he would wait until a special occasion arose for him to wear it, that he was confident in Otis's ability to measure. It was cut from a fine black broadcloth and he'd ordered two white shirts with it. He now took the suit and laid it on the bed and looked at it, then changed out of his work clothes into it, putting on one of the white shirts and then the trousers then the jacket. He buttoned the shirt up all the way to the throat and stood before the mirror to have a look at himself. He looked just like a corpse.

He set his hat on his head, then took the pistols and

stuck them down inside the wide leather belt he had fastened around his waist.

"Time to go to the party," he said, then went on out and closed the door behind him. He wouldn't make it easy for them. He'd take as many with him as would go. They might not get whipped, but they'd least know they'd been in a fight. He went out the back door. Stepping out onto the landing, he could see over the roofs of the other buildings in town. The back stairs were snow-covered, had not been cleaned nor the snow melted off. A brisk wind, sharp as a knife, blew in off the grasslands, cutting down the street and whipping up the loose powdery snow as it went. Little fine gusts of snow like blown sand stung his face as he made his way down the stairs, careful not to slip and fall. Be a hell of a thing if I fell and broke my leg and they just came up and shot me like a horse, he thought.

The stair emptied out into an alley that ran between the butcher shop and the hotel. It came to a dead end at the back of the buildings, where a tall wood fence ran. The other way led to the street. He went up it and paused at the corner, looking around quickly to check the street. He saw them coming out of the café, two and two, with one trailing behind. Dallas and Perk in front, the others, whose names he did not know, falling in behind. They were coming up toward the hotel, their heads down because of the sting of wind-whipped snow. He ducked back, drew one of the pistols, and waited.

They reached the front of the hotel.

"One of you wait out here case he ain't inside. Lon, why don't you go around back case he tries coming out that way. Perk, you and me and Taylor will go in and see can't we just finish this business inside."

Lon said, "Why don't you send one of the others around back?"

" 'Cause I'm sending you, goddamn it."

"Okay then, but don't expect me to stand out there all day freezing my ass off."

"It won't be all day, now, go on."

Jake could hear the shuffle of a man's boots coming in his direction. He pressed himself against the wall of the hotel and waited with his gun at the ready. When the man came around the corner, Jake brought the pistol down hard over his head. Lon staggered, then sank to his knees and Jake hit him again and he toppled over and fell into the snow, his hat all caved.

Jake dragged him farther back into the alley and laid him up against the wood fence, then unfastened the man's belt and jerked it free and used it to tie his hands behind his back and left him lying on his side, making sure his face wasn't buried in the snow. Then he stood, breathing hard from the effort and the tension. By now he figured the ones who went inside would be upstairs already and it wouldn't be but another moment before they discovered he wasn't in the room.

He moved quickly back to the head of the alley and glanced around the corner at the one standing out front. He had a pistol in his hand and was standing there, shifting his weight from foot to foot—nervous or cold. There was a wagon parked just to Jake's left on the street and if he could slip around to the other side he'd have a clear shot at the man in front. The man looked up at the upper windows, as though there was something there to interest him, then he glanced off down the street in the other direction and when he did, Jake stepped out and went around behind the wagon.

The man didn't bother to turn and look back toward the alley and Jake called to him: "Hey!"

Harvey had been standing there, thinking he didn't care for it much— taking orders from Dallas, being left to stand guard out in the cold like some dog or something. It made him edgy, this business, all of it. He didn't mind killing so much as he minded being told what to do. Who was Dallas Fry, anyway, to tell him what to do? Then, too, it was cold and his feet were cold down inside his boots and the sun didn't seem to have no strength to it and what the hell was taking them so long inside, anyway? It was just one man and three of them. Then he heard somebody shout, "Hey!" and he turned to see who it was, thinking it was Lon coming back out of the alley. But when he turned he saw the lawman aiming his gun at him.

"Shit!" It was about the first word he'd spoken in a day and a half and he raised up the pistol in his hand and fired without even giving it a thought and didn't hear the lawman firing his own gun the first time. Between them they fired off four or five shots and it was like a goddamn bad dream or something, he told himself, like his bullets couldn't kill nothing and the other man's bullets couldn't kill him, either.

Bang! Bang! Bang! Bang! Bang!

Then something flat and hard hit him dead center and knocked him backward as if he'd been hit with the head end of a shovel. And right away it snatched his breath out of him and he tried to swallow in more air, but it wasn't doing much good. Down he went and he dropped his gun and lost it somewhere in the snow and was reaching around for it, trying to find it. He saw red drops in the snow, then saw it was his own blood dripping out of him like water dripping from a bad pumphead. Bright and red and wet drops about the size of half dollars at first and he could feel his throat squeezing shut like someone had their hands around his neck, choking him.

Then he just felt like laying down right there and letting go because suddenly he had no strength, and that is what he did. He just lay out flat in the snow and let whatever it was have its way, and the world that was in his head went rushing out and a blackness came rushing in. He tried one more time coughing out whatever it was felt caught in him, then closed his eyes and said to himself, *Well, that's it, then . . .*

Jake saw the cotton batting fly out from the front of the man's coat, then watched helplessly as the man fell and groveled in the snow for a few moments before stretching out straight facedown, then lay still.

There had been other witnesses to the shooting death of the hired hand. They watched from behind plate-glass windows, the first shots attracting their attention. Gus was standing inside the barbershop, him and Carl, the barber, and Will Bird. And from inside the café, the waitress and the folks still there eating their breakfast had been drawn to the window and could watch the scene unfold slantways down the street. Otis Dollar had seen it from his store window, too, looking up the street in the opposite direction, and so had the dentist and his patient, a man with a rotted wisdom tooth, and the lawyer and all the others who had turned Jake down in the fight they knew was coming.

Clara was sitting at her table when she heard the shots. Each one caused her hands to shake so terribly she spilled the coffee in her cup. The girls sat across from her with frightened looks on their faces.

"Mama! Mama!"

Gus said, "Well, he just killed old Harvey."

Will Bird said, "God*damn* I guess he did."

"Yeah, but he's still got them others," Carl said. "I'm betting he don't kill them all before they kill him."

Dallas and the others had kicked in the door to Jake's room, rushing in with guns drawn, and were standing there, looking at old clothes on a bed, when they heard the shots. They rushed to the window overlooking the street in time to see Harvey flop in the snow and the lawman who shot him rise up from behind the wagon, his smoking gun still in his hand.

"God*damn*," Perk said, "he killed Harv."

Dallas smashed the glass and fired through the window and so did Perk. There wasn't enough room for Taylor to join in, so he just stood behind them, trying to see.

The shots splintered wood from the sideboards of the wagon. Jake looked up in time to see where the shots were coming from and something scored his cheek hot and stinging as a branding iron. He stood no chance if he remained where he was. He turned and ran across the street, the whiz and whistle of bullets flying all around him, blood dripping from his face where the bullet had grazed him.

"Let's go!" Dallas shouted.

The three of them ran out the room and into the hallway. That's when the kid, Frisco, pulled the trigger on his dad's old gun, spending the ten-cent shell he'd bought at Otis's store along with some honey for Marybeth to put on her teat. The bullet caught Taylor in the arm and knocked him ass over heels, causing the others to stumble.

"Son of a bitch, I'm shot!" he cried.

Dallas spun around and pulled the trigger and his bullet tore out plaster and wallpaper on the wall near where the kid stood, just as a hand reached out from the open door and pulled the boy inside and slammed the door shut.

"Why that little peckerwood," Taylor cried. "What the hell he shoot me for?"

"He wasn't aiming to shoot you," Dallas said. "He was aiming to shoot me."

"What the hell you grinning at?"

"Nothing," Dallas said, begrudging the boy a small amount of respect. "Get off your lazy ass and let's go."

Taylor pulled off his coat and saw the kid's bullet had gone right into where he'd patched the sleeve on his shirt. When he pulled the torn sleeve open, he saw red bloody meat right above the elbow. It stung like somebody had a pair of pliers pinching on it and his fingers had turned numb. The others were running down the hall, turning the corner and going down the stairs by the time he got to his feet.

"Little bastard!"

Sam Toe heard the shots, as he was shoeing one of the horses that pulled the funeral wagon for Tall John. He had a mouthful of nails and had been idly thinking about Rowdy Jeff, his old partner, the one he had the nightmarish dreams about from that summer the two of them spent alone in high country, tending a sheep camp. *I don't know why I keep thinking about him*, he told himself. *I don't know what there is about it that keeps me going back to that time*. It had plagued him so much he'd been drinking heavily and letting his work slip and now he had these two hearse-pulling horses the undertaker needed shoeing and had had them for a week almost already and just getting around to shoeing the one this morning.

"What the damn hell?" he mumbled. He dropped

down the freshly shod foot of the horse and stood up and saw the marshal running down the street toward him. He spit out the nails.

"What's going on, Marshal?"

"Better clear out," Jake said.

"I don't see myself being run out of own place."

"This is where I'm going to make my stand. You can stay if you want to."

With a snoot full of whiskey, his mind troubled over his strange thoughts about Rowdy Jeff, his work all getting behind, his payments to the bank late on a business he was losing money on every single day, Sam Toe wasn't at all sure what he should do.

Then two shots rang out and Tall John's funeral horse fell dead. It sounded like something smacking leather when the horse was shot. It just fell dead and Sam Toe ducked and said, "Jeez Christ!" and ran through the livery and out the back and kept going with nothing to impede his progress—just a field of snow, deep in some places and less so in others, for as far as the eye could wander. He knew there wasn't a man alive could outrun a bullet, but he sure as hell was going to try.

Jake turned and fired at the three running figures, then ducked back into the darkened interior of the livery. There were lots of places a man could hide, shield himself—stalls mostly—but for how long was anyone's guess.

He knocked out the empty shells and replaced them with fresh loads. Thing was, he couldn't cover both doorways—one at either end—at the same time if they wanted to come at him from both ways at once.

He leaned against a stall. The scent of manure and straw was heavy, thick in the air. Horse collars and old traces hung from the rafters. Horseshoes hung from a spike driven into a post. He could hear the horses out in the corral nickering with excitement having been stirred by the gunfire. He waited.

For a long time nothing, then:

"You come on out or we'll burn it with you in it!" Dallas called. "It don't make a shit's bit of difference to us how it goes. Either way, you're a dead man."

"That's right!" he heard the other one say, Perk, he thought it was, that sharp high-pitched voice of his. "We're good at burning things down!"

Then suddenly several shots rang out and the bullets bounced off metal buckets and chinked wood and he heard one of them say, "That's for you, you son of a bitch, for shooting Harvey!"

Dallas turned to look at Taylor, his sleeve wet and dark with blood and said, "What the hell you talking about you stupid bastard. You and Harvey were never friends."

"We was a little, sometimes, I guess."

Perk grinned.

"Where the hell is Lon, anyway?" Dallas said.

"That son bitch probably killed him too," Taylor said.

"Go around the other side, Perk, cover that back way."

Perk scurried wide of the livery, worked his way through the rails of the horse pen, pushing aside the nervous animals, and climbed out the far side that brought him in view of the rear.

"I've got this covered!" he called to Dallas.

"You gone come out or we gone burn you like a witch!" Dallas yelled again. "Go find a lantern and light it," he ordered Taylor.

"My arm hurts like a son bitch."

"Just do what I tell you or that arm's gone seem like it ain't nothing when I get done with you."

Taylor saw a lantern hanging from a nail on the outer wall of the livery. "There's one," he said.

"Well, go get it," Dallas said.

"I'm aiming to."

Dallas said, "I'm all over this if he comes out and tries to shoot you."

"'At don't make me feel none better."

"Go on, you damn son bitch."

Jake saw the man run past the open door and fired off a shot to no effect.

Taylor reached the wall and took the lantern and ran back and Jake fired again and missed.

"Here," Taylor said. "You want any goddamn thing else, you go get it yourself."

"Light it up."

Taylor said, "I can't hardly use my arm at all. You light it up."

Dallas shook his head disgustedly, reached inside his coat, and took out a match. He struck the head of it off the base of the lantern, then lifted the chimney and lit the wick. It caught and he dropped the chimney back down.

"Now run it up and fling it inside," Dallas said.

"Fuck that."

Dallas cocked his gun and said, "Go on, you son bitch, or I'll shoot you where you stand."

"Shit, Dallas, don't be that way now."

"I am that way, go on."

Taylor judged the run to the open doorway to be about fifty feet or so. He took the lantern in hand and stood up and took a deep breath then started off. A single shot knocked him off his feet.

"What the hell?" Dallas said.

The shot didn't sound like it came from the livery.

He looked round.

A slender, wild-haired, scraggly bearded son of a bitch was standing there with his arm straight out, a smoking gun in his hand, the gunsmoke curling out the end of the barrel.

Taylor flopped around on the ground like a rabbit had its back broke.

Dallas fired off a quick shot at the stranger. The son bitch never even flinched; just stood there sideways with his arm straight out, then moved his gun hand just a few inches and pulled the trigger, just as Dallas pulled his again.

Both men went down.

"What the hell's going on!" Perk shouted from the rear of the livery. He couldn't see the action because the horses in the corral were blocking his view. "Dallas!"

Jake had heard the gunshots, too, didn't know what they were about. Then he heard Perk shouting questions.

"Dallas? Dallas, what the hell's going on?"

Perk ran back to where he'd left Dallas, running around the corral this time instead of climbing through. He got around front and saw Dallas lying faceup, his arms flung out wide from his body, one hand still holding his pistol. He saw off to his right that Taylor was down, still moving, but shot to hell. Then he saw the other fellow, a few feet away from where Dallas was, lying on his side. It looked like a damn slaughterhouse, them down, and Taylor still wiggling around, bleeding.

Jake stepped out into the light.

"Throw it down," he ordered.

Perk didn't say anything, just stood there looking down at Dallas, all that blood pooled out into the snow around him like a red soup spilled.

"Throw it down!" Jake ordered again.

Perk turned slowly and looked at Jake.

"He's dead," he said.

Jake inched forward; they were still a good thirty feet apart in distance. He kept his gun leveled on Perk.

"Drop your piece in the snow, you're under arrest."

"Fuck if I am," Perk said and brought his gun up and both men fired at the same time.

Perk pitched forward and fell facedown forward across the body of Dallas so that they seemed to form a human cross.

Then there was nothing but silence and the brilliance of snow where it wasn't stained with men's blood.

That's when Jake saw the boy, Tig, standing there with his gun smoking. Jake realized then that his own shot had missed Perk and that it was Tig's bullet that had shattered Perk's spine and killed him instantly.

"I guess that makes me and him even," Tig said, then turned and walked away.

28

⁂

FOR WHAT SEEMED like the longest time, there was just the sound of the wind, low and lonesome, crawling over the dead and the living alike. The horses in the corral had gathered along one rail and stood nervously, as though waiting for the next thing to happen. Then, in the quiet, Jake heard water dripping from the eaves of the livery, where the sun had warmed the snow enough to melt it. The water dripped into a large wood barrel Sam Toe kept there to collect it and rainwater in. The wind abated somewhat and there was just the sound of water dripping at first.

He knelt by the unkempt young man with the scraggly beard and saw there was still a bit of life in him.

"Why'd you get involved in this?" he said.

Willy Silk's eyes shifted to meet the lawman's gaze.

He smiled slightly and tapped his pocket and Jake reached in and took out the wanted poster.

"Man in Denver . . . paid me . . ."

"A man named Shaw?"

Willy nodded.

"How come you didn't, then?"

Willy looked skyward for a moment, then back at

Jake and said, "I don't know." Then Willy went to meet his ma, who was just over yonder waiting on him. She and his uncle Reese, his pa, and the angels.

Then Jake stood and saw them approaching, the townspeople, coming on slowly, like coyotes after a kill, coming to inspect the dead, to pick over the bones, to feed and retreat. They came on in twos and threes—the lawyer and banker, the barber and Gus and Will Bird, Otis Dollar and Emeritus Fly, the newspaper editor. Men and women, folks he knew, and some he didn't know all that well.

Their shadows came ahead of them, stretched long over the snow and the sky overhead as blue as any sky that ever was. Blood had frozen on his cheek from where the bullet had grazed him and the wound no longer stung; he couldn't even feel it.

He saw the kid, Tig, walking off toward them, how they stepped out of his way and let him pass as though he were some sort of leper, with that awful face of his and Tig never spoke a word to any of them and they never spoke a word to him.

Farther out he saw a wagon coming across the flat white ground and knew that it was Toussaint. He had come despite every reason against it—he was that sort of man, and Jake was silently glad the killing was finished and that Toussaint didn't have to be a part of it.

They came closer and closer, forty or fifty of them: drunks and ranchers, women and children—all coming to witness the spectacle of death—like a Greek tragedy, where admission was free and make of it what you will once you've seen it.

Then they were circled around him and the dead men and he looked at their faces and saw in those faces all the emotions of humanity, realized that they were neither brave faces nor cowardly ones, neither wise nor foolish.

They were just folks, like any other folks, no better, no worse.

"It's finished," he said. "You all can go home now. You've seen all there is to see. Take your kids and go home. This isn't something they should have to witness."

But for a time nobody moved and he realized they weren't looking at the dead so much as they were at him.

Somebody said, "You did what you had to, Marshal."

Others vocally assented. Most said nothing.

"They deserved it," someone called.

Then slowly they began to drift away except for Tall John and Will Bird, who knew they had their work cut out for them. They'd dig the graves and bury the dead and that would be the end of it. Until the next time.

Jake looked for Clara's face among the crowd.

He was glad to see she wasn't among them.

BILL BROOKS

BRINGS THE WILD AMERICAN WEST ALIVE

DAKOTA LAWMAN: LAST STAND AT SWEET SORROW

0-06-073718-2/$5.99 US/$7.99 Can

When skilled Union surgeon Jake Horn is pursued for a crime he didn't commit, he must abandon his home, his name, and his true calling and instead pick up a gun if he wants to stay alive. On his way to Canada he runs into trouble and finds refuge as a city marshal in a small town in the Dakota Territories.

DAKOTA LAWMAN: KILLING MR. SUNDAY

0-06-073719-0/$5.99 US/$7.99 Can

Billy Sunday, a feared gun artist with a price on his head, is suffering from a fatal illness. But he is determined to reconcile with his daughter before he dies. Lawman Jake Horn may find himself faced with a suicidal duty: to stand side-by-side with a dead man who has nothing left to lose.

DAKOTA LAWMAN: THE BIG GUNDOWN

0-06-073722-0/$5.99 US/$7.99 Can

Lawman Jake Horn recognizes a murdered body when he sees one. But asking too many questions of the wrong people is asking for trouble, and suddenly expert killers are gathering with their sights on him.

Straight-shooting
western action from

J.T. EDSON

RUNNING IRONS

0-06-078419-9 » $5.99 US/$7.99 Can

Texas Ranger Danny Fog could be getting
more trouble than he bargained for when he
kicks in with "Calamity" Jane.

WACO'S BADGE

0-06-078418-0 » $5.99 US/$7.99 Can

In wide-open Arizona outlaws run rampant.
A different breed of peace officer is needed,
and rancher Bentram Mosehan has accepted
the responsibility of organizing a new
Arizona State Police force.

TEXAS KILLERS

0-06-072195-2 » $5.99 US/$7.99 Can

It's Dusty Fog's job, along with the other
members of Ole Devil Hardin's Floating
Outfit, to keep a European crown prince
alive during his visit to Corpus Christi.

COLD DECK, HOT LEAD

0-06-072190-1 » $5.99 US/$7.99 Can

A cardsharp with a conscience, Frank Derringer
comes to the crooked town of Tribune, Kansas,
looking to even a score or two.